THE RAG

MICHAEL CONNELLY

Order this book online at www.trafford.com
or email orders@trafford.com

Most Trafford titles are also available at major online book retailers.

Print information available on the last page.

ISBN: 978-1-4907-7498-5 (sc)
ISBN: 978-1-4907-7500-5 (hc)
ISBN: 978-1-4907-7499-2 (e)

Library of Congress Control Number: 2016910973

Trafford rev.   07/08/2016

www.trafford.com
North America & international
toll-free: 1 888 232 4444 (USA & Canada)
fax: 812 355 4082

CHAPTER I

He was assigned to rat-killing duty in the old Marriott Hotel on the edge of the French Quarter when he found it. He wasn't looking for it. He wasn't looking for anything but rats, and he was doing that only halfheartedly. He spotted it when he was shifting a pile of debris behind what was left of the front desk in the once-ornate lobby of this high-end New Orleans, Louisiana, hotel. It caught his eye because of its colors—pretty colors that he was only vaguely familiar with.

There was no color in his world, at least no pretty colors. Everything was gray—his uniforms, his barracks, even the New Orleans landscape was just a dull gray—or so it seemed to Inmate 6024. He held the colored rag he had found in his filth-encrusted hands and glanced around the wrecked lobby to see if he could spot anything similar that the rag might have been torn from. Even in the poor light that filtered in from the smashed windows, he could see there was nothing of color remaining on the ground floor of the Marriott or suspect anything similar was on the upper floors.

This building, as well as most of the others in the historic Vieux Carré area of New Orleans, had been looted many years ago. Even the buildings that had survived the devastation of Hurricane Katrina had not been immune from the human insanity that had occurred a few years later. Inmate 6024 knew there were a few buildings in good condition in the area, but they housed the bosses and were basically self-contained units that contained luxuries that inmates and ordinary citizens were only vaguely aware of.

Since he was only a grade 5 inmate, he knew he would never be allowed inside one of those grand lodgings. Only grade 1 inmates were allowed the "privilege" of working for the bosses. Not that it really mattered to him. In fact, very little mattered to one whose brain barely functioned above the survival-mode level. He sometimes had flashbacks of vague memories of a time when he was another person entirely, a time when things did matter, but now he could not remember what those things were. He couldn't even remember what he had done to warrant the bosses putting him in the New Orleans detention camp.

All he really knows these days is that the bosses give him food, clothing, a bed, and his daily pills. They also gave him some very powerful marijuana to smoke every night to make him feel good and forget about his plight. Inmate 6024 is not even sure who the bosses are. He just knows that they work for the Socialist Republic of America (SRA), often simply referred to as the state, and they are in charge of everyone and everything.

Inmates were not allowed to have any personal possessions, and this colorful rag would be considered a personal possession and confiscated when he returned to the compound. He would be severely punished for such a transgression. Yet he felt compelled to keep it, so the question is how would he sneak it in? For some reason, he felt the answer might lie with an older man in the detention center that he only knew as Inmate 4031. A man who had seemed to develop a special interest in him, almost like the father he only vaguely remembered.

The old man once told him that he knew of a section of the high chain-link fence surrounding the compound that was not covered by the security cameras. He said that if the young man ever wanted to sneak something important into the compound, he just let the elderly gentleman know, and he would meet him as he passed that part of the fence and a small item could be handed to him through the fence. Inmate 6024 decided to try that so he hid the rag in the hotel, knowing that he would be assigned the same duties at the same location the next day.

That night, he confided to his fellow inmate about what he had found and his desire to get it into the prison. The man became very agitated when he heard the description of the rag and vowed to help. Everything went as planned the next evening, and that night, after lights out, the two men met in the bathroom where they could see if they stood under reflection of the outside lights that were shining through the small windows.

As the older man unfolded the rag, he said something that stunned the young man, "Before I give you this and we talk about what it means, I want you to tell me your name. My name is Ray."

The young prisoner hesitated because he knew that the use of real names was forbidden. Yet he instinctively trusted this man, so he said, "My name was—is James. I think I remember my parents calling me Jamie."

"OK, Jamie. Now we can talk as men instead of as robots created by our captors. How long ago did you stop taking the mandatory drugs?"

The young man stiffened up and hesitated again. He really didn't know this man, so he lied, "I am still taking the pills as required."

"No," replied Ray. "If you were still on the full dose, you would have not even have noticed what you found at the Marriott, much less asked me to help you sneak it into the compound. I just stuck my neck out for you, so it is time we trust each other. I suspect you have reduced the amount you are taking, and that is why you are not showing any of the obvious signs of withdrawal."

Jamie still hesitated, but he knew Ray was right. He had put himself at risk, and so he deserved the truth. "I had a dream several weeks ago. I think it was about my father and mother, but I could not remember the details. Then I realized that I could not even remember what they looked like or any of the details about my life before I came here. I want to remember, and something told me that it was the pills that were keeping that from happening, so I started pretending to take them and spitting them out. I have continued to use the marijuana, and so far, I can still not remember much, so getting off the pills is not enough."

"It takes some time," replied Ray, "but you obviously have regained the ability to think in the present, and the memories will return. Now, let's talk about this piece of cloth."

They talked for a few hours, and Jamie felt it all slowly to come back to him. He had not recognized the rag immediately, but it had seemed vaguely familiar. Ray told him that it was the flag of the United States of America, which was what their country had been named for almost 250 years while it was a constitutional republic. The flag had been banned even before the new government took over and the country was now named the Socialist Republic of America.

The USA had not died overnight. It took years of effort by people calling themselves progressives who believed that they were the elite and were destined to control the lives and destinies of everyone else. They were totalitarians following in the footsteps of the Communists, Nazis, and Fascists who had gone before them in other countries.

The campaign was steady and insidious. They started by taking control of most of the news media outlets and turning them into propaganda organs for the progressive political agenda. At the same time, they gradually took control of the universities and then of the entire public school system. The education system was transformed from a place where students learned how to prepare themselves to live in the real world and be productive members of a free society to an agent for reeducation.

Instead of being taught to honor their country and its history, students were trained to believe that freedom was evil and individualism and personal responsibility had to be replaced by government control of all aspects of life. Personal freedoms were replaced by collectivism and subjugation of individuals to the will of the state.

Freedom of speech and expression was replaced by political correctness that allowed the government to monitor and control what people said, did, and even thought. The Judeo Christian religious foundation of the United States came under massive attack. Freedom of religion was replaced by freedom from religion.

That was all they had time to talk about that first night, and Jamie had many questions that Ray said would be answered later.

CHAPTER II

Ray and Jamie met every night for at least an hour, and much more of the story was revealed to the young man. He learned that the progressives had driven the vibrant American economy into the ground, putting millions of people out of work. This often left families with their only choice to survive being the reliance on government programs that were specifically designed to make them dependent upon and subservient to the government.

They soon learned that they had to surrender all their freedoms to the government if they wanted to stay on the federal dole. Any resistance to the government was severely punished. One of the requirements was for people to surrender any firearms they might own. This was part of an ongoing effort to disarm the American people by destroying the right to keep and bear arms guaranteed by the Second Amendment of the Constitution.

The disarming of the citizens had started slowly but had gained steam over the years. Throughout history, dictatorships had only been successful if they had succeeded in disarming the indigenous population. In the United States, various restrictions on firearm ownership had been passed by Congress over the years. But firearms ownership in the country had actually grown as more and more Americans realized that they needed to protect themselves from the rising crime and violence and also possibly from their own government.

The progressives saw that more proactive action had to be taken, so they took a page from Adolf Hitler's playbook. Hitler had been named chancellor of Germany in 1933 and immediately began efforts to disarm the German people, beginning with the military veterans. They represented the greatest threat to a dictatorship in Germany, and the progressives in the US government saw the same potential threat from American military veterans.

Using the Veterans Administration that was supposed to be an agency to take care of and protect veterans and using other federal agencies, the government instituted a program to declare veterans incompetent to handle their own financial affairs and based on that declaration also declare them too mentally ill to be allowed to own, purchase, or possess firearms and ammunition.

After all, as members of the military, American veterans had taken an oath to "protect and defend the Constitution of the United States against all enemies, foreign and domestic." That oath did not end when they left the military, so there were millions of highly trained veterans who posed a danger to the emerging dictatorship and therefore they must be disarmed.

Despite resistance by many veterans, the program was expanded to include senior citizens receiving Social Security benefits and then to others receiving federal or, in some cases, state benefits. Yet many people refused to voluntarily turn in their firearms, particularly in the face of increasing violent crime by gangs and left-wing political activists who mysteriously had all the weapons they needed.

Gradually, the progressives had succeeded through persistent propaganda in dividing the American people according to race, religion, and income. People were told they were entitled to have what other people had worked for even if they were unwilling to work themselves. Criminal activity was excused, and people who entered the country illegally were allowed to stay even if they committed crimes.

However, all this had not proved enough to bring down the United States completely. Something else was needed—something catastrophic. It was an electromagnetic pulse (EMP) attack on the United States that did not go exactly as planned. In fact, it went terribly wrong.

CHAPTER III

Ray was an enigma, even to his captors. His full name was Raymond Thibodeaux, and he had been raised in the southwest part of Louisiana by a Cajun mother and a father of Irish and Cajun ancestry. He was just over six feet tall, stout, and a lot stronger than he looked. His weathered appearance made it hard to gauge his age. All that his captors really knew about him was that he was an accomplished chef who had once owned one of the finest restaurants in the New Orleans French Quarter.

He had been arrested several years earlier when he was caught feeding some members of the patriot resistance late one night in his restaurant. This was an action punishable by death for everyone involved, and the members of the resistance who were caught were immediately executed. However, Raymond was spared because some of the administrators of the detention center were aware of his reputation as a culinary artist. The food they received in their dining hall was much more plentiful and far superior to the meager rations provided to the prisoners, but its quality of preparation left much to be desired.

Ray was seen as the solution to this problem, so the plan was not to sentence him to death but to put him in the detention center and assign him to supervise the preparation of meals for the prison guards and administrators. His captors were convinced that they knew everything they needed to about Raymond Thibodeaux, but they were wrong. Before Raymond had become an accomplished chef, he had been a Green Beret major in the US Army. The problem for the feds was that all the military records in the Pentagon had been destroyed in the EMP attack. So there was no way for the government to identify the military veterans and keep track of them. That was not the way it was supposed to have worked out.

The EMP attack had actually been coordinated by the progressives in the US government. The President had worked with the rogue governments in North Korea and Iran that had obtained nuclear weapons and essentially hired them to make the attack so it could not be traced back to the federal government. The attack was supposed to be limited and only target the states that would be the most troublesome such as those in the South, the Southwest, and the upper Midwest and Northwest.

This would cause the electric grids to be shut down in those areas for months and possibly years. Chaos would be the norm. The US economy would be brought to its knees, and everyone would have to rely on the government for survival. It would control the supply of food, water, medicine, and fuel and limit those supplies to cities and groups of people that professed complete loyalty to the new government.

The fact that there would be food riots in the big cities and millions of people would ultimately die in the chaos from starvation and lack of medical care would not be a negative but would get rid of the undesirables such as Christians, conservatives, gun owners, and members of minority races who could not be used as cannon fodder but might drain the system of resources. In other words, it didn't matter how many died or who they were as long as the elitists remained in control and did suffer from any deprivations themselves.

Before the attack took place, leftists in the government secured massive amounts of weapons, ammunition, food, water, and medical supplies. The military equipment had been placed in secure areas for years, but while every effort had been made to purge the military of those men and women who might be loyal to their oath to protect and defend the Constitution against all enemies foreign and domestic instead of being loyal to the new dictatorship, there were still many members of the military that could not be trusted. They were isolated from sensitive positions that might provide them with access to heavy weapons and equipment.

The new regime was also aware that the twenty-three million veterans in the country would be a major problem. Government efforts to disarm them and other elements of the population had been somewhat successful, but many people had managed to hide their weapons. The plan was to use the government databases of veterans and Social Security recipients to keep track of those who were suspected of still owning firearms or would otherwise oppose the government. The limited EMP attacks were designed to spare Washington DC and surrounding areas from being affected and would therefore maintain access to these databases, and the regime could proceed to arrest and incarcerate all these people immediately following the attack.

The key to the success of the limited EMP attack was to set the nuclear devices on the missiles to detonate at lower altitudes. It was supposedly well established that a nuclear bomb detonated at 250 to 312 miles in the atmosphere over Kansas would shut down the entire electric grid in the United States. To prevent this from happening, it was decided to set off detonations at 200 miles.

To a certain extent, it worked. Most of the red states lost their power while many blue states such as California and Oregon out west, the New England states, the states in the Northeast, and Washington DC were mostly spared. Unfortunately, for the government, the EMP attack produced an unintended consequence. It created an Internet virus that completely destroyed all databases including those stored in the cloud. Government computers no longer had the names and addresses of veterans or any other potential gun owners.

At first, it was not considered a serious problem, at least in the case of veteran records, because they had all been transferred to flash drives that were locked in metal safes that would be safe from an EMP attack. A military team of computer specialists led by a US Army captain had been assigned to transfer all veteran data to these flash drives. However, when government agents went to recover the flash drives and their data, they found nothing. Everything had been erased, and the soldiers in charge of them had disappeared. So had the records of veterans like Raymond Thibodeaux, and the government therefore thought they had nothing but an outstanding chef in detention.

CHAPTER IV

As Ray continued his nightly meetings with Jamie, the trust between the two continued to grow, and more was revealed to the young prisoner. First, Ray told Jamie more about the piece of cloth that Jamie had first thought of as the rag. It was more than just the flag of the United States. It was, in fact, one of the most important flags in American history. The day after the September 11, 2001, attack on the United States, some New York City firefighters raised an American flag amid the rubble that had once been the twin towers of the World Trade Center.

That image was an iconic one for the American people who were initially united against the radical Islamic terrorists who had launched the 9/11 attacks. The flag was eventually removed and replaced by a permanent flag, and the original one was supposed to have been stored by the city to be used later in future ceremonies honoring those who died in the attacks.

However, it was later discovered that the original flag had been stolen and replaced by another flag. This was determined by the fact that before the firefighters had raised the original flag, they had written the date of the attack on its edge. The replacement flag did not have that date. An intense investigation was launched, but while the thieves could not be identified, it was thought that the flag had been sold to a private collector.

It was ultimately determined that a key suspect in the purchase of the flag was a millionaire businessman from Saudi Arabia. He had business and real estate interests all over the world, including in the United States. However, it was also suspected that he was tied in to several Islamic terrorist organizations including the Muslim Brotherhood. That meant that if he acquired the flag, it was as a jihadist trophy, not a symbol of American heroism.

It was also suspected by Ray that the flag could not be easily smuggled out of the country and was kept at one of the residences used by the Muslim businessman. One such residence was a suite of rooms at the New Orleans Marriott Hotel. It would probably have been in the hotel's safe that was broken into by looters after the EMP attack. The significance of the flag would not have been recognized by the looters, and the flag was discarded, to be found years later by Jamie.

Ray told Jamie that the flag needed to be returned to the American people, in particular those still resisting government tyranny. Ray knew where at least one such group could be found, and it was time to have Jamie meet with some of the other members of the cell of American patriots that existed in the detention center. There were only seven others because the men who were able to overcome the drugs and function normally without the guards seeing though their charade had to be incredibly strong and resourceful.

Ray had an uncanny ability to spot such men and recruit them into his small circle. They had been planning an escape for some time, and now with the addition of Jamie and the discovery of the iconic flag, Ray had determined it was time to act. All seven of the men actually worked for Ray in the prison. He had freedom to operate that was granted to few other inmates.

The detention center was located at the original location of Tulane University on historic St. Charles Avenue. All the dorms and classroom buildings had been converted to house the inmates, and the other buildings had been set up to house the guards and administrators of not only the detention center but the regional headquarters for the ISA (Internal Security Agency). All the nearby houses, many of them historic landmarks, had been destroyed, so there was a clear buffer zone and field of fire around the prison.

Included in the buffer zone but outside of the fence surrounding the prison were several large fields that had been converted to gardens. The guards wanted more than just the bland rations supplied to them. They wanted to have fresh vegetables and spices as well as fresh meat and eggs. So one of the fields was filled with vegetables such as green beans, corn, potatoes, lettuce, tomatoes, and other items to augment the incredible menus that Ray was producing. The other one was where the produce was grown to feed the pigs and chickens that were kept in adjacent pens. There were even a few cattle kept on the premises; some were dairy cattle to provide milk, and the others were raised for their beef.

Ray had been put in charge of all this, and he was allowed to handpick the men who tended to the gardens and cared for the animals. That meant that he and some of the people who worked for him were allowed to be outside of the fence for most of every day. Five of Ray's recruits worked in these areas, and the other two worked for him in the kitchen. Unfortunately, only three of them were housed in the same barracks as Ray and Jamie, so there was no way for all of them to meet together at the same location.

At their usual meeting time and place, Jamie was finally able to meet these three men. The first of these men Jamie was introduced to was a forty-six-year-old named George Carson. He was a small wiry individual who appeared to be a bit of a nerd. He wore glasses, had a pale complexion, and just looked weak. He was, in fact, a former Navy SEAL who had been an active fighter in the war on terrorism. He left the navy when it was being turned into a shell of its former self and had become a police officer in his hometown of New Orleans. He now worked in the detention center kitchen with Ray.

The second man was a tall, muscular, and handsome black man named William Jackson, who had been a captain in the Second Ranger Battalion of the Seventy-Fifth-Ranger Regiment of the US Army. He had been a highly decorated fighter in the war on terror, earning a Silver Star and Bronze Star for bravery and two Purple Hearts. He had resigned his commission when he had seen the military becoming a vehicle for social experimentation and political correctness instead of an organization of dedicated men and women who wanted to defend their country. He had also ended up back home in New Orleans as a police officer. He had been assigned by Ray to work in the garden.

The third individual was also a military veteran named Frank Hansen who had been a young lieutenant in army intelligence and had become disgruntled when he found out that reports he and other intelligence analysts were submitting to their superiors about the growing strengths of various terrorist groups were being altered to understate the actual threats. He was the youngest of the three men and was a large-boned white male with rough features and facial scars received during a training accident while in the army.

Frank had not become a police officer in New Orleans. He had received his commission as an army lieutenant after completing ROTC at Louisiana State University and earning a degree in engineering. After leaving the army, he had gotten a master's degree and gone to work for the city of New Orleans as a supervisor of the agency that maintained the levee system surrounding the city. He did not actually live in New Orleans but resided in the city of Kenner in Jefferson Parish, Louisiana. It was there that he had become a reserve officer in the Jefferson Parish Sheriff's office.

In the cases of all three men, they had been arrested by the government not because of their military backgrounds but because of their work as local law enforcement officers who had refused to violate their oaths of office and pledge allegiance to the new dictatorial government. Therefore, they were considered a threat to the new order and needed to be reeducated.

Ray and his group had been planning an escape for a long time and were fairly sure that they could get out of the camp, but they needed a way to get out of the city. The inclusion of Jamie in the group gave them something they had not had before: eyes in the city itself.

CHAPTER V

Jamie has successfully stayed off the drugs and had gained Ray's complete trust and that of the other three men he had met. He was still on rat-killing duty at the Marriott and surrounding buildings, and that was a plus for Ray and his team. The bosses eventually wanted to redo the Marriott to create luxury condos for some of the higher-ranking government officials, so the plan was to clean up several blocks around the hotel.

The hotel was located at the corner of Canal Street and Chartres Street right on the edge of the historic French Quarter. The location was important because it was only a few blocks away from the headquarters of the Eighth District of the New Orleans Police Department on Royal Street Both George Carson and William Jackson had been stationed at that location. Even before the EMP attack, both men had seen that the advance of the progressive government was going to lead to the destruction of the United States. So they had joined with several other like-minded officers and had started stashing confiscated weapons and ammunition in a nearby location.

The weapons had been seized from gang members and other criminals and were supposed to be logged in to a central location and stored until they were ultimately destroyed. The officers had falsified the records so that not all the weapons were put into the central registry of the department. The location where the weapons were stashed was across Royal Street and just a half block away from the police station. They were in an antique store that occupied a historic two-story building that dated back to the early 1800s.

It had been the residence of one of the wealthy New Orleans families and included a beautiful courtyard. Off to one side of the courtyard, there had been a carriage house that had been bricked in years before to provide additional space for the store to hide some of its finer antiques until they were displayed in the public areas. The entrance was hidden behind a movable bookshelf that contained old books. George Carson was friends with the owner who was also a patriot and readily agreed to have weapons stored there. The owner, an elderly Jewish man, had unfortunately later been murdered when he tried to protect his property against the looters who ransacked the city after the EMP attack. They had ransacked the store but had not found the hidden room, so George had every reason to believe that the weapons were still there.

This meant that in order to have a successful escape, Ray and his men had to accomplish three goals. First, to get out of the detention center without being immediately detected; second, to get to the location of the weapons and get as many as they could carry; and, third, to find a way to transport themselves and the weapons out of the city. Then they had to successfully execute the plan.

Jamie's job was to find a route from the camp to the weapons cache that would avoid government patrols and also to locate some form of transportation and a safe way out of the city. Jamie always had a good memory at least until he was subjected to the government's drug regimen. Now the memory was coming back, and he was starting to think about how he had ended up in federal detention.

His father, Ben Donnelly, had been an army officer, and the family had moved around a lot. When his father retired, they ended up living in Dallas, Texas. His father had been a stern but loving man who was a patriot and had tried to raise Jamie and his two brothers, Matthew and John, to be patriots. He had been successful with the brothers, but the younger Jamie was a rebellious teenager.

As his father and his mother, Jean, became more involved with the efforts to resist the changes the Left was forcing on the country, he and Jamie had often argued. Ben had started writing and speaking and had eventually become the executive director of a group called Americans to Restore the Constitution. On the other hand, Jamie had been taught by his liberal high school teachers that the Constitution was an outdated document written by slave owners to perpetuate racism and tyranny. He bought the party line completely.

Eventually, his father's organization had been shut down by the government, and authorities were monitoring Ben and Jean and their two sons, Matt and John. Jamie was not aware of these developments since when he graduated from high school, the government had sent him to Tulane University in New Orleans. He was seen as a brilliant student who was loyal to the new government, and it was felt he could be trained as a psychologist who could assist in the manipulation of behavior and the retraining of individuals who resisted the new order.

Jamie had eagerly accepted the opportunity despite the objections of his parents and had gone to the federally controlled university. He had not talked to his parents since that time and was not aware that they had fled Dallas one step ahead of the federal police. They had never been located. All this had occurred about a year before the devastating EMP attack. After the attack, the university had been virtually shut down. Classes were canceled, but a select group of students, including Jamie, were going to be assigned to the federal police operating in New Orleans for some specific on the job training.

Following the attack, most of the cities in the United States had descended into absolute anarchy. Food and water shortages, the loss of power, and the lack of local police protection led to widespread looting and other crimes including rape and murder. Local authorities tried to do what they could to protect lives and property but were limited by federal restrictions that required them to swear allegiance to the new government and do what they were told even if that included looking the other way when the feds told them to.

Jamie was assigned to ride with one of the federal police squads that were patrolling the city. This way, he could get a feel of what was going on in the streets and see who was being arrested and for what reasons. Then he would help decide if the prisoners could be reeducated or needed to be simply incarcerated. During the ride along, Jamie saw humanity at its worse. Mobs were looting stores and then setting fire to them. People were being beaten and robbed in the streets or in their own homes.

Yet the federal police were seemingly making no attempt to break up the riots or arrest the looters. Instead, most of the people being arrested were business or home owners who were trying to protect themselves, their families, and their livelihoods. If the officers saw someone resisting the looters with a firearm or even a knife, it was they who were arrested. Their homes or businesses were being searched and all weapons confiscated.

In fact, the officers Jamie was with had a prepared list of names and addresses of people that they were picking up. It didn't seem to matter if they were actively resisting looters or just hiding in their homes. Their houses were being raided and the homeowners led out in handcuffs. This was all being done pursuant to the order that had been handed down by the government several years ago outlawing the private ownership of firearms. It had been difficult to enforce at the time because few people were willing to voluntarily surrender their guns. In addition, many local law enforcement officers refused to kick in the doors of their friends and neighbors and violate their rights under the Second Amendment to the Constitution.

However, the federal government had been preparing for this for years. The National Instant Criminal Background Checklist (NICS) maintained by the FBI was supposed to have been for the purpose of preventing convicted felons, known illegal drug users, and people who had been adjudicated to be mentally ill to the point of being a danger to themselves or others from legally purchasing firearms. Everyone who wanted to purchase a gun from a federally licensed firearm dealer had to first fill out a form that included their names, addresses, Social Security numbers, and other personal information. The form was then transmitted to the FBI that did a background check and then approved or disapproved the purchase.

Under federal law, the form was then supposed to be destroyed within seventy-two hours. This had stopped being the case under orders from the president years before. All the information was transferred to computers and eventually flash drives, so there was a permanent record of Americans that legally owned guns. It was portions of that list that were being used against the people of New Orleans, following the devastation of Hurricane Katrina in 2005.

However, Jamie noticed something odd. Many of the looters had firearms, and while some were being disarmed by the feds, others were ignored. They appeared to, in some cases, being in charge of the looters and rioters. What was happening appeared to the young student to be orchestrated by the federal police to encourage the anarchy.

There were some people who were using firearms to defend their homes or businesses and refused to surrender to the federal authorities. When that happened, members of SWAT were called in, and the resisters were usually gunned down after a short firefight. In some cases, families had banded together to defend whole neighborhoods, and they were also attacked by the feds and ultimately killed or arrested.

Jamie tried to ignore what he was seeing or justify it by telling himself that the feds were just doing what was necessary to restore order, and questioning their tactics was not part of his job description. Yet when he later interviewed some of the people that had been arrested, he began to realize that the majority of them were not dangerous criminals but ordinary American citizens just trying to survive the chaos.

His job was clear: decide if the people he was interviewing were to be placed in regular prisons for indefinite terms or be reeducated to accept the new order. He was not empowered to consider if they were guilty or innocent of any crimes that might have been charged with. That was not his job because they were all considered to be guilty. Jamie had heard about the concept of due process of law provided in the Constitution but had been taught that it was meaningless in a progressive society where obedience to the government was imperative and the feds decided who were friends and who were enemies. So in effect, Jamie was the judge, jury, and potential executioner of the people that were sent to him. Many of those sent to prison instead of reeducation camps did not survive for long. They were tortured, starved to death, or just outright executed.

Jamie had received a thorough indoctrination from the government about the ways that this new order would benefit everyone. Yet now he was having some serious misgivings about what he was witnessing. He was beginning to wonder if his father and mother had been right all along, and what Jamie had considered their radical conspiracy theories had not been crazy after all. He continued to do his work for the government, but his concerns would not go away. Especially when he saw more and more men, women, and even children being arrested for crimes that only involved refusing to obey government edicts or even just saying something that was critical of the government.

He ultimately made the mistake of confiding his concerns to his best friend and roommate, Frank Madison, who was a longtime resident of New Orleans and had started Tulane University with Jamie. Frank listened to what Jamie had to say and then told him that he was seeing the same things and having the same concerns. The next day Jamie was arrested and charged with being an enemy of the state. As he was led out of the dorm by the federal police, he was horrified to see Frank shaking hands with the federal agent in charge. He had been betrayed.

He remembers little about what occurred after that. There was no trial. He was evaluated by federal authorities and sent to the detention center where he was drugged and put to work for the state.

CHAPTER VI

Now that Jamie's memory was back, he was determined to help Ray and his team escape, so he could join them in the fight to restore freedom in America. He also hoped, although he knew it was a long shot, that he might find his family—if they were still alive. He owed them a major apology.

He spent the next several weeks watching the area surrounding the Marriott. His captors were confident that Jamie was under their complete control and would do nothing but what he was told to do. They were sure that he was simply a human robot who was no longer capable of independent thought. He was part of a crew that was taken by guards every morning to the Marriott. They were checked in with the area guard post on Canal Street and then were then left to their own work until the evening. The government did not have enough personnel to assign a guard to each inmate or even a crew of inmates.

So every evening at dusk, the inmates were programmed to report back to the guard post and were then accompanied by a single guard back to the detention center. This was not because the feds were afraid inmates might try to escape but because many of them were so heavily drugged that they might simply get lost if left to find the detention center on their own. However, the guard just walked the inmates to within side of the main gate and left. That was how Jamie was able to sneak the flag through the fence at the blind spot found by Ray.

During his time alone in and around the Marriott, Jamie was able to mentally record the times that the regular patrols went through that area of the French Quarter. The patrols usually consisted of five heavily armed men, and they always took the same routes at three-hour intervals. Few people still lived in the

French Quarter because homes, hotels, and apartment buildings had been heavily damaged during the looting and riots a few years earlier. However, some high-ranking government officials occupied the luxury homes and apartments that had survived and could be restored. The patrols were there to protect them.

Since Jamie was only in the area during the day, he could only assume that the patrols operated in the same way at night. If that was, in fact, the case, he could lead Ray and the other men successfully to the building where the weapons were stashed without encountering the enemy. Then the problem would be finding a way to transport the weapons and the men. There were abandoned vehicles throughout the area, but they had been disabled by the EMP attack and could not be started. Even if they could be fired up, the fuel had long ago been removed for use in vehicles that could run.

There were many running vehicles at the district headquarters of the federal police, but it would be virtually impossible to steal any of them. However, Jamie had found another possibility. Prior to Hurricane Katrina in 2005, the city of New Orleans had a population of almost 500,000 people. That had been reduced significantly after the hurricane, but by 2015 the population had rebounded to around 369,000. However, the combination of the EMP and the subsequent riots had caused thousands of people to flee and thousands more to be killed. Now the population had been reduced to just over 50,000 and approximately 10,000 of those people were prisoners of the federal government.

Most of the other people either worked for the government or had at least sworn allegiance to the government. They all had to be fed, and the new government's system of collective farms set up around the state could not begin to meet the needs of the city. Thus, food was heavily rationed, particularly to both the general population and the inmates in the detention center.

Much of the food was imported from Mexico and countries in Central and South America and was brought to the port of New Orleans by small ships that used less fuel than large container ships. The food was offloaded and stored in a large building on the Mississippi River that had been built in 1891 and once been the home of the Jackson beer brewery. Now it was a warehouse for food. The best of the food went to government bosses; and the rest was distributed to the federal police, the general population, and the detention center for the inmates.

The food was transported around the city in a fleet of unmarked vans. The vans were not marked since if the population knew that there was food in them they would often be hijacked despite the fact that an armed guard rode with each of the vehicles. Jamie knew that if Ray and his team could steal several of these vans from the motor pool next to the warehouse, they could transport the escaping men and the weapons they had secured.

This was just one part of the plan since the group then had to get out of the city. Driving out would be almost impossible since while most of the men were locals and knew the streets, they had no way of knowing where patrols or checkpoints might be set up. Therefore, Jamie was also assigned to check the Mississippi River for a large boat that could be stolen and that could take the men and weapons upriver in the dead of night.

There were many tugboats and fishing vessels tied up to the wharfs at night, but the tugs posed several problems. First, they had crews onboard twenty-four hours per day, so the boats would be on call to assist ships coming into the port day or night. Secondly, a tug could not move without specific permission of the harbor master and would be easily spotted and monitored.

The fishing boats were different. The crews did not work for the government. They were able to come and go at will. When they returned with a catch, the captains had to check in with the harbormaster, and two-thirds of their catch was taken by the government. They were allowed to sell the other third at the farmer's market in the French Quarter. That was the way they made their livelihood. The normal routine was for a boat to sail from New Orleans downriver into the Gulf and spend several days fishing.

It would then return to the city with its catch, and the crew would spend a day or two with their families onshore before going out again. No one stayed onboard, and when they did sail, it was often late at night. That meant they would be perfect for Ray's escape plan. The flaw was that there was no normal schedule followed, so Jamie had to identify more than one possibility. It took several weeks of observation, but he finally found three large fishing boats that would fit their needs, and at least one of them would be available on any given night they chose for the escape.

CHAPTER VII

The plan was starting to come together, but it was a clearly a long shot because of all the elements involved. First, the group the Ray Thibodeaux had put together was housed in three separate facilities in the detention center. They would therefore have to orchestrate three separate escapes from three separate locations. Then they would have to get out of the center, avoid the French Quarter patrols, and steal several vehicles from the old Jackson brewery, retrieve the weapons, proceed undetected to the wharf, and steal a fishing boat. It seemed like an impossible task, but the men of Ray's team were willing to risk all to escape the federal prison and rejoin the fight for their country.

Then Mother Nature intervened. Many of the prison guards were from Syria, brought in to reinforce the Americans who had turned on their country. They spoke Arabic and believed that no one else could understand them. However, since Ray had been a Green Beret, he had been required to learn a second language, in his case, Arabic. Thus, one August day he heard some Syrian guards discussing the fact that a hurricane was approaching New Orleans.

The forecasting was not as accurate as it used to be when the sophisticated computers were online, but basic radar was still operating, and it showed a category 3 storm coming toward the city from the southeast Gulf of Mexico. It was expected to hit the city directly in two days in the early morning hours. Winds in a cat 3 storm would range from 111 to 130 miles per hour with higher gusts possible. The storm surge would be nine to twelve feet, so the combination of heavy rains and a rising tide in the large lakes around New Orleans would cause some flooding. It was also a sure thing that the city's power system that relied on a combination of solar-powered and gasoline generators was iffy at best and would probably go down.

The guards were discussing that possibility and the action that was going to be taken. The detention center had backup generators that were either solar powered, gasoline powered, or a combination of the two. Regardless, they had limited gasoline and were not sure how the generators that were solar powered would perform in hurricane conditions. So the plan was to only turn on a few generators at a time. This would provide limited lighting of the compound at night, but the guards were not overly concerned since the inmates were so drugged up that escape did not enter their minds. That would allow the guards to have sufficient power to light the quarters of the guards and administrators and make sure they got hot food, regardless of how long the blackout lasted.

Ray found all this very interesting, and it could prove to be a game changer for their escape plan. One major concern Ray had always worried about was the fact that his men were housed in three separate dorms. This meant that they would have to escape from these multiple locations, meet a predetermined location, and breach the fence. The hurricane provided Ray with a plan to get everyone together in one location without having to escape from individual dorms.

With a hurricane coming in, the fields of fruit and vegetables and the animals would have to be secured and protected from the storm. Ray planned to suggest to his superior, the mess hall administrator who was a federal employee, that he would take the men who worked for him in the fields and several members of his kitchen staff to place covers over the plants and move the animals into shelters. He also strongly suggested that he and his men and the guard assigned to them spend the night in the tool shed that was a solid brick structure and should survive the storm. That way, they could monitor the plants and animals during the storm and resolve any problems that might occur. He believed that this idea would be accepted because of the importance of fresh food to the administrators of the prison.

The second major concern for Ray was the fact that while they could steal vehicles and transport the weapons to the boat on the river, they would need to return the vehicles to their original location, but he was afraid that someone would note that a boat was missing before Ray and his men could get to their intended destination. The hurricane could solve that problem. Instead of returning the vehicles, they could be driven into the river. The missing boat would probably initially be attributed to the storm. The logical assumption would be that it had torn loose from its moorings and either sunk in the turbulent river or run aground somewhere downstream. A search for it would not be a priority in the aftermath of a major hurricane.

On the other hand, once it was discovered that some inmates were missing from the prison and that several federal vehicles were also missing, a search would be launched for the vehicles. That would be a good diversion for the team since hopefully no one would connect the escaped inmates to a boat torn from its moorings during a storm. Of course, making it upriver in a fishing boat during a hurricane would not be an easy task, but the winds would be at their back, and one of the members of Ray's crew had been a chief boatswain's mate in the Coast Guard and later an accomplished ship's pilot on the Mississippi River. If anyone could successfully maneuver a boat up the river during a hurricane, it would be Jason Arnaud, a short swarthy Cajun originally from Ville Platte, Louisiana.

The detention center's administrators readily agreed to Ray's plan to protect their food supply. The plan was now in place, and over the next twenty-four hours all the members of Ray's crew were notified of the final version of the plan. The next day they were all moved to the fields to prepare the plants and animals to survive the hurricane. The exception was Jamie. He had never been assigned to this type of work, and if Ray were to request his presence now, it might raise suspicion, so Jamie went out to do his usual duties and signed in at the guard post near the Marriott at the end of his shift. Then when the guard escorted the men within sight of the detention center and left them, Jamie slipped away to hide in a nearby park where he would be joined later by Ray and the rest of the men.

It was correctly assumed that with the hurricane approaching, the guards at the detention center would not have time to launch a search for a single man who had probably just been disoriented and wandered off. They believed if he survived the storm, they would soon find him after the storm had passed. However, the rest of the plan ran into trouble.

Ray and his crew that cared for the gardens and animals were usually accompanied by a single guard every day. This was because while other inmates were believed to be taking the mind-altering drugs, Ray had been allowed to stop taking them. The prison administrators wanted Ray to be at his best when preparing their meals and did not want him to forget their favorite recipes. They were not aware that he had stopped taking them long before he received their permission.

They trusted Ray but could not afford to be found negligent in their duties, so a guard was always assigned, and it was usually the same guard: an amicable heavyset white former truck driver named John Magee, who had sworn allegiance to the new government and taken the only job available to him, that of prison guard. He and Ray had become friendly, and this bothered Ray because he knew that John would have to be killed and his body hidden to cover the escape for as long as possible. A plan was already in place to have Magee overpowered during the storm and killed.

On the day that the storm was scheduled to roll into New Orleans, Ray and his men prepared to move outside of the main compound and into the gardens, but they were shocked to learn that there were two more armed guards assigned to accompany Magee. He recognized both of them as men who usually guarded the barracks where Ray, Jamie, and three other men in the unit were housed. Now Ray's crew would have to kill three guards in order to make their escape. It was not impossible but would be considerably more dangerous, and the whole plan could fail.

As they went about their work of covering the plants in plastic and staking the plastic down, as well as moving the animals into prepared shelters, Ray spoke to all of them about how they could execute the taking out of the three guards and their ultimate escape. However, they never needed to execute the plan, which was supposed to occur as they were being escorted to the shelter after completing their work.

Although the full force of the storm was not due to hit the city until after midnight, the outer bands of wind and rain from the storm started coming in during midafternoon. Ray and his crew had started work early in the morning, but with several thousand plants and animals to be protected, it was tedious work. By the time the winds started increasing and the rain was pouring down in the afternoon, much of the work had been completed, but it was dusk before everything necessary had been done.

Now the critical moment had arrived for Ray's men to attempt to overpower the guards and initiate the escape plan. The inmates were lined up to be taken to the shelter when something unexpected happened. Sergeant Magee took Ray aside and had a lengthy conversation with him. After that conversation, Ray approached his men and gave them a one-word command: abort. This command was unexpected and disturbing to the men to say the least, but they all trusted Ray completely so they had no choice but to obey.

Once inside of the of the brick building where they were protected from the howling wind and rain, Ray revealed to his group what Sergeant Magee had told him. Magee had stated that he was a patriot that had been forced to become a guard because his wife of thirty years was seriously ill. Medical treatment of any kind, and especially medication, was severely limited when it came to the regular population and was in short supply even for employees of the federal government. The best was reserved for the bosses, but since Magee knew that he could get at least some treatment for his wife as a federal guard, he took the opportunity.

The so-called treatment proved to be seriously inadequate, and his wife had died several years ago; but instead of leaving federal service, Magee had decided to try to do what he could to help others escape captivity. He had originally been a guard in

Baton Rouge, Louisiana, the city where his wife had died that was only sixty miles north of New Orleans. He had been transferred there shortly after his wife's death. Two other guards had been transferred with him: the very two men who were inside the shelter with Magee and Ray and his crew. Their story was different from Magee's. They had freely pledged their allegiance to the new government and applied to be prison guards so they could assist in the reeducation of their countrymen to get them to accept the new order and become compliant.

In fact, the two men, Tim Johnson and Jerry Calhoun, were former army intelligence officers who were members of the Louisiana National Guard. Many members of the Guard had gone off the grid with their families and had taken significant amounts of equipment to prepare to fight to take their country back from the usurpers that had stolen it. The job for Johnson and Calhoun was to infiltrate the prison system and find out what techniques were being used to control the prisoners and identify the former military members that they could help to escape and join the fight.

The prison administrators had assigned all the barracks guards to monitor the prisoners carefully to watch for any inmates that were showing signs that they were not taking their medications and were coming out of their zombielike state. Johnson and Calhoun were very good at such detection, and it didn't take long for them to identify two men who were part of Ray's team. They were also aware that Ray was not required to take the drugs and that he was conducting clandestine meetings in the barrack's bathroom.

Of course, all the barracks contained listening devices to record the conversations and activity of the prisoners, and that included any activity in the bathroom. Ray had been sure that this was the case, and it had only taken him a few minutes to find the device in the bathroom hidden behind a toilet. It was easy to cover it with a towel when Ray held his meetings, and when they listened to the recordings, Johnson and Calhoun were aware that something was being done to mask conversations, but they did not report it or try to keep it from happening. This was because Sergeant Magee had informed them of who Ray really was and he suspected that an escape was being planned.

That was what Magee had told Ray when he pulled him aside. He had also told Ray why he had known his true identity, and that was what convinced Ray that Magee and the other two guards were allies. Now he had to convince his worried and skeptical men. He informed him that Sergeant Magee had never directly met him; it turned out that Magee had also been a Green Beret, and he knew of Major Raymond Thibodeaux by reputation, and he and his A team were assigned to an ultrasecret mission in Afghanistan along with the three other A teams in his company. They would all be under command of Major Thibodeaux and were briefed on the mission by him.

That was the only time Magee had seen him, except for briefly as the teams moved in on their objective. The mission had been completed, and Magee never saw Ray again until he was transferred to the center in New Orleans. He knew that Ray had not recognized him because he had just been one of thirty-six Green Berets that had briefly been under his command. Magee had put on considerable weight since then, so Ray did not initially make the connection; but when Magee described in detail the operation that had happened in Afghanistan, Ray knew he was telling the truth. Ray conveyed all this to his men and his belief that the guards could be trusted to join them, but he could tell that the situation had made his crew uneasy, so he gave them a choice.

"I've told you what I think, but it is up to you," said Ray. "Sergeant Magee and his men will let us go without them and take off on their own. Obviously, they can't stay around and tell their superiors that they were overpowered and we escaped on their watch. They would probably be executed on the spot."

Sergeant Magee stepped in and told the still-skeptical inmates that that he and his men had something that might help in that decision. They had several duffel bags with them, and they opened up and gave each of the men in Ray's group a loaded Glock 19 pistol and two extra clips of ammo. This sealed the deal, and Ray prepared his men and their new allies to move out.

However, something more had to happen before they could move. The building they were in had no windows and was normally only used during the day so they would have to open the door to see what was happening outside. It was now dusk, and since the sun was setting, all the security lights would be on. They cautiously cracked open the door to their shelter, and when they did, they saw that the wind had gotten stronger and the rain was getting heavier, but the lights were still on in some of the buildings including the one they occupied and the compound. They would have to wait and pray that these lights would eventually go out.

Then shortly after eight thirty, the light in the building went out; and when they checked outside, they saw that the lights in the detention center were also dark. It would just be a matter of minutes before the backup generators would be started, and while they would not illuminate the area where Ray and his group were located, it was still time to move. While Magee and his men had brought a change of clothing with them, it was decided that they needed to stay initially in their federal uniforms so that in the unlikely event that they did run in to a federal patrol in the storm, Magee could convince the patrol leader that they were escorting the inmates to the river to help secure the boats there.

CHAPTER VIII

The escape plan was now put in motion, and the group headed out to join up with Jamie in the nearby park. They moved out in the standard military patrol formation. Captain Jackson took the point; he would lead the patrol and be the first one to make contact with Jamie who knew him. He would explain why there would be men in their group who would be wearing federal police uniforms. Once this meeting took place and he had talked to Jamie, he signaled the rest of the patrol to move up. When everyone was together, Jamie said he had reconsidered the original plan and offered an idea that would change the plan to make it better.

The original idea was to steal several vans, load them up with the weapons from the secret cache, and then offload the weapons to the boat and set sail upriver. The vans would be driven into the river so that when the feds realized that there had been an escape they would start looking for the vans. Jamie had seen a flaw in the plan while the fishing boats came and went at will: no fishing boat captain would have taken his boat out to sea when there was a hurricane coming in. Therefore, the feds might quickly determine that the missing boat could have been stolen by the escaped prisoners.

Jamie suggested that after he led the group to the area where the vans were parked, he and two other men proceed immediately to the wharf where the boat was located. They would pick out several other boats moored in the same area and cut them loose so they would drift out into the river. Once loose, the boats would be battered by the current that would try to force the boats downriver and the hurricane winds that would be trying to push them upriver. They would eventually either run aground or possibly sink, but either way, it would deflect suspicion that the prisoners had used a boat for their escape.

Ray now knew for sure that he had made the right choice when he had included Jamie in the group. The young man had a good head on his shoulders, and this proved it. Ray immediately agreed to the plan, and Jamie led the men out of the park toward the French Quarter. The fury of the storm was rapidly increasing, so they would have to move quickly, and that would not be easy since the power was out throughout the city. It was pitch black, but Magee and his men came to the rescue once again. Prior to going on duty watching Ray's crew, Magee had checked out three pairs of night-vision goggles for the alleged purpose of being able to hunt down any inmate that tried to escape in the storm.

Jamie was given one set, and he would be in the lead accompanied by Captain Jackson who would also have a set of goggles. Jamie would be looking for the landmarks that would keep him on the right track while Jackson would be looking for any signs of the enemy and danger. The third set was worn by Ray, so he could lead the rest of the men who would all be walking with a hand on the shoulder of the person in front of them. This would hopefully keep someone from getting lost, because if that happened, that person would be on his own and the rest of the team would not have time for a search.

It took more than an hour for the escapees to reach their destination, and the men were all soaked to the bone. However, as expected, they had encountered no federal patrols. The motor pool where the vans were kept was fenced in, but Ray had known about this since Jamie had scouted it out. The gate was heavy and locked with a padlock and chain but was not that high and could easily be scaled by the highly trained men in Ray's unit. They would then hot-wire three vans after disabling the GPS. They would crash through the gates with the vans, and the noise would be covered by the raging storm.

As they prepared to steal the vans, Jamie and his small group moved out for the wharf. Ray's men took only a few minutes to secure the vans and proceed to the location where the weapons and ammunition were stored. The building had remained abandoned since it was looted. George Carson led the men to the bookshelves that were hiding the door to the secret room. He had been given the code to the locked room by the now-deceased owner, and he opened the room easily. They had taken several flashlights from the shed they had been hiding in at the detention center, and when they lit up the room, they found it was still filled with all the weapons that George and his comrades had originally placed there.

In addition to the standard assortments of hand guns and semi-automatic rifles, there were also various automatic weapons such as Uzis, AK-47s and M16s. The various gangs in New Orleans had been well armed, particularly the ones connected to Mexican or Colombian drug cartels. Some also had connections to Islamic terrorist organizations; so in addition to firearms and ammunition, there were also several cases of hand grenades, three cases of C-4 explosives, and over three dozen RPGs.

The vans that the crew had stolen had already been loaded with food for the next-day delivery, and they had to be at least partially offloaded so that there would be room for the munitions and the men. They kept as much of the nonperishable food they could because they would need it for their journey through enemy lines. That necessitated leaving some of the weapons behind along with the extra food, but there was no other option available.

CHAPTER IX

It had only taken Jamie and the other men with him a few minutes to reach the wharf where the boats were tied up. Jamie pointed out to Jason Arnaud the three boats he thought they should choose from. Jason quickly checked each one out by boarding them—inspecting the engines, the radar, and radio equipment—and then checked the hulls and cargo holes. He settled on a one-hundred-feet-long boat with a twenty-two-feet breadth. It was a snapper boat, so it was designed to fish closer to shore for red snapper. It was not particularly fast, but it was sturdy and had a shallow draft so was perfect for navigating the Mississippi River and Louisiana bayous.

Another plus was that it had almost half a tank of fuel. That was unusual since fishing boat captains usually drained their tanks when a storm was coming in so that if the boat was torn loose from its wharf and collided with another boat it would not explode. However, these were not ordinary times, and diesel fuel was scarce. Offloading the fuel into tanks on the dock made it much more vulnerable to theft than keeping it in a locked tank on the boat. Arnaud's inspection was as complete as it could be with the use of just a small flashlight that he kept shielded. The boat was named the *Marie L*, probably for the famed voodoo queen Marie Laveau who had once ruled New Orleans through a combination of magic and blackmail. Jason decided to rename the boat *Freedom Runner*.

In the meantime, Ray and his crew were moving as quickly as possible to get the food unloaded from the vans and then reload them with weapons and ammunition. The process was not helped by the increasingly heavier rain and wind, but they all knew that time would be running out unless they made it to the boat and were headed upriver by midnight at the latest. When the vans finally moved out shortly after nine thirty, it was slow going since they obviously could not travel with their lights on.

However, it would have been much slower if the three drivers had not had the night-vision goggles that Jamie felt were not needed by his team because he knew the route to river well and there was abundant lightning from the storm to show the way. Fortunately, the streets of New Orleans were empty since everyone knew better than to venture out during a powerful hurricane. When the vans finally reached the wharf, Jason directed them to the *Freedom Runner*, and the process of transferring the food and munitions into the hole of the boat started immediately. On fishing boats, the cargo holes were usually filled with ice; so after the fish were caught, they would stay as fresh as possible during the trip back to New Orleans. It was not a pleasant place to work in, but to these Americans who were preparing to make a run for freedom, it smelled like roses.

As Ray's crew unloaded the vans, Jamie and Jason were joined the third member of their group, a young man named William "Billy" Jordan, a former soldier in the Louisiana National Guard who had been arrested for allegedly trying to hide guard weapons from the federal police in Lake Charles, Louisiana. He had made his living initially working offshore on oil rigs in the Gulf of Mexico until the progressives decided to shut down the oil companies and replace them with government-run companies.

Jamie, Billy, and Jason had fire axes they had taken from various boats and went to the other two boats that were to be cut loose to confuse the authorities. They carefully chopped through areas of the wharf where the mooring lines were tied, so it would look like the boats had been torn loose by the winds. They didn't cut them all the way through immediately. The final cuts would be made when the *Freedom Runner* was ready to sail.

That occurred at eleven nine, ahead of the self-imposed schedule. As Jason fired up the boat's dual engines, the other men cut loose the two decoy boats and destroyed the wharf around where their own boat was moored. Then they jumped on the

Freedom Runner as the boat headed up the river. They had already driven the empty vans into the muddy-churning waters of the river.

The river was choppy and the current was strong, but the wind was still behind them, so they were moving slowly but steadily. This allowed Jason to use the night-vision goggles to watch the river ahead for any signs of sandbars that would often shift location even when there wasn't a storm stirring the river up. The pilot also had to watch out for any other obstacles in the river, and he couldn't take a chance on turning on the boat's running lights or searchlight.

The crew quarters below deck were designed to house six men. There were five small sleeping cubicles for the crew, a somewhat larger cabin for the captain, and a galley where all the food was prepared, the men were fed, and also where the crew held their nightly poker games. With the addition of Magee and his men, there were twelve in Ray's group; and so even with Jason at the helm, the crew area was crowded. The men did not care about the crowded conditions because this was the first time in hours that the escaped prisoners had been in a dry place.

They found some dry clothes that belonged to the fishing boat's crew but decided not to change immediately since they were just going to get wet again before this night was over. So everyone was soaked to the bone and cold, but they did find some slickers to wear over their wet clothing. Most of the weapons, ammunition, and food had been stored in the boat's hole; but each man had kept an automatic rifle and pistol in case they ran into trouble. As the propane stove in the galley started to heat some rations so the men could have a hot meal, several others went topside to assist Jason.

Jamie was one of them, and he volunteered to man the open stern with his weapons and night-vision goggles so he could look for any possible enemy patrol boats that might come up behind them. Two other men moved on to the enclosed bridge to help Jason watch the river in front and on both sides of the boat. At this point, most of the men were still in the dark as to where the boat was headed. Only Ray and Jason knew, but now that they were on the river, the destination was revealed to all them.

CHAPTER X

The initial destination was an area outside of Donaldsonville, Louisiana, a city of approximately 7,600 people on the west bank of the Mississippi River in Ascension Parish. It had a mixed population, but many of the people living in the parish were Cajuns. Among them were Ray Thibodeaux's relatives including his first cousin Daniel Thibodeaux. Ray had been raised in Ascension Parish on a two-thousand-acre plantation that had been in his family for generations. Its primary crop was sugarcane although his family also raised some beef cattle and thoroughbred horses that they raced on the tracks like the one in nearby Lafayette, Louisiana.

Ray had been raised on the plantation with his younger sister, Jennie, who had tragically drowned one hot summer day while swimming with friends in the bayou that ran through the property. She was sixteen years old at the time of her death, and she and Ray had been very close. The whole family was devastated by the loss, and Ray took it particularly hard but knew that his life must go on. He had just graduated from high school and had enrolled at LSU to study agriculture.

He had also enrolled in the army ROTC program and when he graduated became a second lieutenant with a two-year active duty requirement in the army. While in ROTC, Ray had gone to airborne school and qualified as a paratrooper. He had also been a member of the elite Bengal Raiders, a unit in the LSU ROTC program that received training from US Army Rangers. Ray had excelled in the program, and when he was commissioned as an infantry officer, he immediately applied to ranger school and was accepted. He also excelled there; and when he graduated, he was offered the chance to go to special forces school in Fort Bragg, North Carolina.

Ray had to think long and hard about this opportunity. If he successfully completed the training and became a Green Beret, it would require an extension of his active-duty requirement. While his parents had been proud of him for becoming an army officer, they had thought that after serving two years of active duty, he would serve the rest of his commitment in an army reserve unit near the plantation and would take over the day-to-day operations of the family business. His parents were getting old and tired, and they needed his help.

On the other hand, Ray had always had a dream of defending his country as a Green Beret and had expressed this to his sister shortly before her death. Years before, he had watched the John Wayne movie called *The Green Berets*, and that was the basis for his desire to serve his country as an elite soldier. Jennie had emphatically told him to follow his dream despite the wishes of their parents. Then his sister had died, but Ray had not forgotten what she said but also was concerned about his parents.

However, Ray had come up with a plan. His cousin Daniel had been an offshore oil field worker who had suffered a serious injury and had lost three fingers on his left hand when a chain used to stabilize a drilling rig had broken loose and hit him in the hand. After the accident, he could no longer work in the oil fields and had been living on disability, but Ray knew of his cousin's abilities and work ethic, and he convinced his parents to hire Daniel to manage the plantation. He and his family could live in the guesthouse on the property that had once been an overseer's cottage but had been greatly enlarged.

It would help both Daniel's family and Ray's parents, and Ray could continue his career in the army. His parents understood how important that was to him, and they readily agreed. Daniel and his family were relieved and grateful for this opportunity, and while Daniel's lost fingers kept him from working in the oil fields, he was still capable of doing everything that needed to be done on the plantation.

Ray served in Operation Desert Storm, and by the time the attack occurred on 9/11, he was not only a Green Beret captain but was the executive officer of a Green Beret company. This followed several years of being a highly successful A team commander who had directed several covert missions. He and his company were ultimately heavily engaged during the invasion of Afghanistan, and Ray received the Silver Star for leading an operation that took down a key Taliban commander and his base. Shortly thereafter, Ray had been promoted to the rank of major. Four years later, when his company was in Iraq, the company commander was killed by an IED, and Ray became the new commander. His company went back to Afghanistan several more times, and during one of those times, he led the raids that Sergeant Magee had been a part of.

Within six months after that action, he had received the tragic news that his father had died of a heart attack. He was granted leave to return home to attend his father's funeral. When he got to the plantation, he received another shock: his mother, who had always been a robust woman, was frail and ill. He learned that she had been diagnosed with terminal lung cancer and had only a few months to live. She also was living with the guilt of believing that worrying about her was what had led to Ray's father's heart attack.

Ray was devastated. His parents had been all he had left of his immediate family since the death of his sister. Ray had spent virtually all his time in combat zones since 9/11 and had really no opportunity to meet a woman and establish a relationship. He had never married although he had always hoped to eventually because he really wanted to have a family. He felt he could not abandon his mother in this time of need, so after they returned from the funeral and his mother had been helped back to her bed, he sat with her for a long time.

He took her frail hand in his and still tried to see the beautiful woman who had been his mother when he was growing up. She had been a classic Cajun beauty with dark hair that framed the features of a tanned face with thin lips and a perky nose. She had always been a hard worker, first in the fields of her family's farm and then later in the fields of the plantation that belonged to her and her husband. Her body had always been fit and shapely, and she had aged well while keeping her natural beauty.

Now she was just a shell of her former self, and Ray felt he could not leave her, so he told her that he was going to resign his commission as an army officer and take care of her. He explained that since he had been on active duty for over twenty years, he would get good retirement benefits. His mother listened patiently and then squeezed his hand tightly and looked deep into his eyes.

"You will do no such thing, young man," she said. "You do not understand how proud your father and I have been of you. You are fighting for our country, and you are an American hero. You are our hero. Daniel and his family will take care of me while you return to the fight." She could see Ray's hesitation, so she continued, "You have three days before you have to fly back to join your unit. So I want you to go to the barn, get your camping equipment and fishing gear, and go to your special place on the bayou. Take whatever food you need from the house and spend a couple days there fishing and talking to your father. He will be with you. He will convince you that I am right."

Ray agreed, and it was a therapeutic two days. This had been the spot where he and his father had often come and where he had often spent time on his own. It was the times out in the woods, whether he was alone, with his father, or his Boy Scout troop, that he felt closest to God. So he fulfilled his mother's wish, set up camp, and started fishing. He quickly felt the peace he had always experienced at this spot, and he felt the comforting presence of his father. So he relaxed and fished. He snagged two nice catfish, cleaned them, fried them with a sliced potato over a campfire, and enjoyed his meal along with more than a few shots of scotch.

He knew his parents were indeed proud of him and his dedication to his country. He was also proud of himself because he believed he was a good soldier. He also knew that he was becoming increasingly concerned with the state of the military and the government that controlled it. His own unit had been subjected to unnecessary danger because of ridiculous politically correct

41

rules of engagement ordered by the president of the United States. High-ranking commanders who had objected to the rules had been quickly purged from the military.

It was the hardest decision he ever had to make, but he knew that he could do nothing to save his mother while he could do things that would help save the men under his command and hopefully contribute to saving his country. He also knew it was what both his mother and late father wanted, so he met with his cousin Daniel the next morning and told him that once his mother passed away Ray was the sole heir and would inherit the plantation.

"I want you and your family to continue living on the plantation and move into the main house, but you will no longer be just an employee. You will be a full partner in the plantation. You will draw your regular salary, and since you will be doing all the work, you will also receive 50 percent of the net profit. This will be permanent," he told Daniel. "I will eventually retire from the army but have other plans for my future. I would like to be able to visit here whenever I can, but the plantation will be yours."

His young cousin was stunned and extremely grateful, and he assured Ray that he would take good care of the plantation. Ray had spent the rest of his time entirely with his mother and then gone back to his unit in Iraq. He was home again within six weeks to bury his mother, but by then, his Green Beret company was in Fort Benning, Georgia, for rest and for "retraining."

CHAPTER XI

Over the years, Ray had watched helplessly as his beloved US Army had become a poor shadow of its former greatness as had the rest of the military. Budget cuts had led to the loss of benefits and pay raises for troops. Even worse, the size of the military had been greatly reduced, and there were shortages of up-to-date equipment so that the branches could not always be effective fighting forces.

He had also watched helplessly as the areas of the Middle East that he and his comrades had fought so hard to liberate were seeing the rise of terror group like ISIS and a resurgent al-Qaeda. The whole region was falling apart, and thousands of so-called refugees were flooding into Europe and even the United States and Canada. A significant number of them were working for the terrorist groups. This was leading up to increasing terrorist attacks around the world, and the government in Washington DC didn't seem to know what to do, so they did very little. In fact, in some ways, it seemed to be allying with these enemies.

Ray's unit was redeployed to Afghanistan but only tasked with training members of the Afghan security force. That is what they had been doing when Ray's parents had died. Now they were at Fort Benning for additional training. Ray was stunned by what the retraining consisted of. His unit and other Green Beret units were being trained for operations in the United States against potential "domestic terrorists."

The training materials that were marked "top secret" designated these potential domestic terrorists as members of civilian militia groups, members of the NRA, and other groups supporting the Second Amendment to the Constitution, people in right-to-life groups, Tea party, and other conservative organization members.

Most disturbing to the Green Berets, all military veterans were on the list.

Their training involved kicking down doors in a fake US city to practice arresting and, if necessary, killing American citizens. It also involved training in interrogation techniques that were long banned when it came to jihadists and other terrorists but were now apparently perfectly acceptable for members of the NRA and other Americans. Ray could tell that the other members of his team were as uneasy about this as he was.

What they were being prepared to do violated several federal laws and, of course, the Bill of Rights of the US Constitution. It would also require him and his men to violate their oath of office. That was something that none of them were willing to do. Unfortunately, Ray had become aware that some of the other men going through the training did not feel that way.

There were several groups that were mostly kept separated from the Green Beret teams. They were not special forces or even army rangers. They wore the uniforms of members of the United States Army, but many spoke very poor English and appeared to be from Middle Eastern or African countries. They were part of what was being called special contingency units and even wore unique patches that some of Ray's team thought closely resembled the ISIS flag. The members of these special units seemed to be very enthusiastic about the training they were receiving.

Once their training was done, Ray was approached by several members of his company who were scheduled to be up for reenlistment and had decided not to re-up. Two of his officers also informed him they were resigning their commissions and leaving the army. Ray understood completely and did not try to talk them out of it. He knew that there would be many more such conversations down the road.

In fact, Ray had briefly considered resigning but decided he owed it to his men to stick it out as long as they could. All that changed about six months later when Ray heard from an officer up the chain of command that was a friend of his that all members of the active military officer corps were going to be required to take a new oath. It would not be to protect and defend the Constitution of the United States like their current oath but an oath to protect and defend the new government and its supreme leader. Anyone who refused to take the new oath would be dishonorably discharged and get no benefits.

Ray passed this information on to his men, and all his officers immediately resigned their commissions. Ray did the same because he knew he could not take the new oath. However, Ray was not prepared to give up on his country. He needed to find a way to make a living, so he would be in a position of connecting with the public and monitor the pulse of the American people. He knew that what was coming was not what he and most Americans believed in.

Ray started his quest by going home to the plantation where he again took his camping and fishing gear and went to his beloved spot on the bayou. He spent the first few days just fishing during the day, dining on his catch every night and then staring into the campfire, and asking for guidance from his father and his God. Then he started considering his options, and something his mother used to say to him came back over and over. She had been a renowned Cajun cook and had taught Ray everything she knew. She was highly impressed with how fast he caught on and how good he was. She told him on numerous occasions that he could become a famous chef if that was his desire.

Instead, Ray had become a soldier serving his country. Now he realized that if he turned to cooking as a profession, it would provide him with the opportunity to indulge his passion for cooking, interact with the public, and have a perfect cover for preparing to resist the growing oppression by the government that he saw just over the horizon.

CHAPTER XII

Ray met with Daniel to inform him of his decision. He was going to move to New Orleans, go to culinary school, and become a chef. The arrangement with his cousin would continue, and Ray told him that he had previously drawn up a will leaving the plantation to him should something happen to Ray. Daniel had done a good job with the plantation, and he had made a substantial amount of money for both his family and Ray. When that was combined with the money Ray had saved over the years and with his pension, he hoped to open his own restaurant in New Orleans.

His dream became reality much faster than he could have hoped. He enrolled in the New Orleans Culinary Institute, one of the finest in the world, and began his studies. He was the oldest person ever to enter the school, and his much younger classmates teased him about his age until they realized that Ray was an extremely talented cook and that they could learn from him. Ray kept his background as a soldier a secret from everyone except the school's director who was also a veteran.

Ray felt that if his true identity was known, it would interfere with his ultimate plan, and that was not just to own a restaurant. Ray breezed through the school and graduated with honors. He was offered several opportunities by top restaurants in New Orleans but turned them down and did what he wanted: opened his own place. It was small and located in a building that had once been an ornate private residence on Decatur Street in the French Quarter. It had later become an excellent and highly popular Irish pub but never reopened after the devastation of Hurricane Katrina.

It had a well-equipped kitchen and a spacious dining area, so it had been leased several times by individuals who opened restaurants, but none were able to live up to the standards required by the discerning New Orleans restaurant diners who demanded only the best. Ray was undeterred by these previous failures and paid top dollar for chefs to assist him in the kitchen and for a waitstaff that would provide impeccable service to his customers. He also hired some young men and women in the neighborhood to hand out thousands of fliers in the neighborhood to both locals and tourists in the French Quarter.

Ray knew that tourists would come and go, so the clientele of a successful restaurant in New Orleans, known to the locals as the Big Easy, had to be based on the city residents who once they tried the restaurant would keep coming back and recommend it to their friends. Ray decided to capitalize on his Cajun ancestry and named his place Thibodeaux's Fine Cajun Cuisine. It took several months, but his plan for his restaurant worked.

It quickly gained a reputation as a top eatery. Ray and his staff gave the people of New Orleans the fine dining and service they expected from a great restaurant. It was going well for Ray but not for his country. He was seeing it deteriorate before his eyes. Basic freedoms were being lost; elections were being stolen and in some places were not even being held. Progressives had gained control of city and state governments, and where such control existed, it was fully supported by the federal government and the newly formed federal police.

New Orleans had been a city controlled by liberal Democrats for years, and the politicians who were in charge were more than willing to let the federal government take over their city. The federal agents were aggressive in shutting down free speech and dissent and confiscating firearms from private citizens—when they could find them. Resistance to this new tyranny was quietly springing up all of the country, and New Orleans was no exception.

However, Ray seemed only interested in the fame of his restaurant, and he cultivated the liberal politicians in the city, particularly the highest-ranking officials of the federal administration and federal police. He gave special discounts to them and always catered to their every need. He also led them to believe that he was supportive of the progressive agenda, and he would keep his ear to the ground and report any dissenters to them.

This was the hat he wore in public, but in private, he had quickly made contact with the largest resistance group in the city and was actually gathering information for them. By listening in on conversations of the federal officials who tended to speak freely in his restaurant, particularly after a few predinner drinks and liberal servings of fine wine, Ray found out who was being targeted and what his customers' plans were for crushing the resistance.

He would pass this information to the resistance leaders during their after-hour meetings at the restaurant. This continued even after the EMP attack. Most of the restaurants in the city had been forced to shut down since power was very limited. That problem was almost immediately solved for Ray since his establishment was so popular with federal and local officials. The government provided him with a heavy-duty generator and plenty of fuel so he could keep his restaurant operating for the pleasure of the feds even while the rest of the city was disintegrating around them. This continued for months, and Ray got more valuable intelligence that saved the lives of some members of the resistance who had been identified as enemies of the state and were able to escape before they were picked up.

Unfortunately, disaster was soon to follow because one of the militia members was a traitor, and he told the federal police about the secret leadership meetings that were taking place at Ray's restaurant. A week later, the feds raided the restaurant and arrested Ray and all the militia leadership. It was devastating for the New Orleans militia, and most of the top leaders were executed within a few weeks. The rest were sent to the detention camps along with other members of the militia who were also arrested in a massive sweep throughout the city.

Ray was among them, but at the time of the raid, he had not been in the meeting but instead in the kitchen, preparing several trays of food for the militia leaders. When interrogated, the militia leaders claimed that Ray had just rented them the restaurant and did not participate in the meetings or know what they were about. The feds did not really buy that story, but it gave them the excuse to detain Ray and turn him into their private chef as the cook for the people who controlled the detention center and the city.

CHAPTER XIII

Now Ray was on his way home again, back to the family plantation outside of Donaldsonville, Louisiana. He was coming home on a stolen fishing boat, and he was on deck, searching for the entrance to the bayou that ran through the family plantation into the river. The bayou had always been wide and deep and was used by fishing boats belonging to local families that would sail down to the Gulf of Mexico to catch fish and shrimp for restaurants in the cities of Donaldsonville and Baton Rouge.

Ray hoped that the presence of another fishing boat moored along the bayou would not be noticed until they could unload their cargo and make plans to transport the team and what weapons and ammunition they could to their final destination in Texas. Ray also hoped that Daniel might help him procure some type of transport for his men and some of the food, weapons, and ammunition. The rest would be left with Daniel to be hidden or used as necessary to defend his cousin and the rest of the large extended Thibodeaux family.

The hurricane that was now moving through New Orleans was turning to the west, so the winds and rain upriver at Donaldsonville were not nearly as severe as those still ravaging the coastal cities and towns of Louisiana. However, visibility was poor, so both Ray and Jason Arnaud were using night-vision goggles to scan the west bank of the river. It was the experienced sailor and river pilot Jason who spotted the bayou and slowly turned the fishing boat into it. However, they almost immediately encountered a totally unexpected problem.

A half mile up the bayou, there had been a famous Cajun restaurant called Robichaux's Landing. Ray had assumed that it had been long closed but saw it lit up in the distance. This was definitely a problem because they would have to sail past the restaurant to get to the landing at the plantation, and Ray knew that the boat would be spotted by anyone in the restaurant, and he had no idea who might be there. He immediately ordered Jason to reduce speed and put the boat as close as possible to the shore of the bayou without running it aground.

Once this was accomplished, the engines were stopped, and two team members dropped the boat's anchor to keep it from drifting. The boat was equipped with a small dingy and several rubber life rafts, and Ray decided to use one of the latter to transport him and two members of the team to the shore. He had to approach the restaurant to find out what was going on. To accompany him, he chose William Jackson, the former army ranger captain, and George Carson, the former Navy SEAL.

They landed on the shore of the bayou, tied off the raft, and started to move through the thick woods. For the first time in many years, Ray smelled the delightful odors of pine and fir trees, and it only took him and his men a few minutes to reach the clearing surrounding the restaurant. They were immediately forced to withdraw a few yards back into the tree line when they spotted several armed guards patrolling the perimeter of the clearing.

Ray had a pair of binoculars he had taken from the boat and used them to examine what was going on in the restaurant. He could tell right away that from the relaxed atmosphere, the music, and the laughter that it was probably a *fais do-do,* which is the Cajun name for a dance party. Ray had to smile because he appreciated the fact that only Cajuns would use a hurricane as an excuse for a party. As he scanned the faces in the room, he realized that he knew many of the older participants at the party. Some were his cousins, and others had been high school classmates and lifelong friends.

He finally spotted his cousin Daniel, but the problem was how was he going to let Daniel know he was outside and get him to meet him in private, particularly with the area being hammered by rain and some wind. He couldn't just walk into the party because he did not know everyone who was there. He needed another way to reach Daniel, so he took a closer look at the three heavily armed young guards that were patrolling the area. He was pleased when he recognized one of them as Daniel's oldest son Johnny, a young man who had always admired Ray and he had been close to.

As he watched his young cousin and the other two guards make their rounds, Ray realized that every few minutes Johnny was in a position behind the restaurant that was out of sight of the other two guards. Ray moved through the tree line and got into position so he could get the young man's attention. The sound of his voice would be muffled by the wind and rain, so no one but Johnny would hear him. He used hand signals to get his two comrades through the woods and then stopped them so Johnny would not be spooked by the sight of three men instead of just one.

As Johnny got near Ray's hidden position, he called out to him, "Johnny, it's your cousin Ray. I need to speak to your father in private. It's important."

Johnny froze, but he recognized the voice and then his cousin when he stepped out of the woods and could be seen in the lantern light that was emanating from the restaurant. Johnny was surprised and delighted as he shook his older cousin's hand. No one in the family had heard from Ray since just prior to the EMP attack, but they all knew about the chaos in New Orleans, so they feared that Ray might be dead.

The young man acted quickly; he told Ray to follow him, and he led him to a covered and screened-in porch behind the restaurant kitchen. Once Ray was in hiding, Johnny went back outside and told the other two guards he had to go inside for a few minutes to use the bathroom. Once in the building, he pulled his father aside and told him where to find Ray. Then he returned to his guard post, unaware that his every move was being watched by two of Ray's men. Ray had told them what he was doing, but in case something went wrong, they were to immediately return to the boat and head out into the Mississippi River to try to get upstream to another location where they could hide out.

They were ordered specifically not to try to rescue Ray if he was captured. A firefight would reveal their presence and compromise the safety of the rest of the crew. Ray had made George Carson his second in command, and he and Jason Arnaud knew where Ray was planning to ultimately take his men, so they could proceed without him.

In fact, Ray's meeting with Daniel went off with no problems. He briefly told his cousin where he had been and how he and the others with him had escaped. He told Daniel that they needed to get the boat safely up the bayou to a secure location where they could offload the food and weapons and hide them. They also needed a place to stay until they could set off on their trek to their final destination. He told Daniel that they were hoping to get some form of transportation to help them along even if was just some donkeys or horses to be used to help carry their loads as they walked to their destination.

Daniel may have only had a high school education before he went to work on the oil rigs, but he was highly intelligent and resourceful. He let Ray know that he and several of the other members of the family had formed a secret militia and all the people attending the fais do-do were involved in the militia. They could all be trusted. They knew that there would probably be no federal patrols in the area during the storm, so they decided to enjoy themselves and throw a party. He also informed Ray that, in fact, they had very little contact with the feds who only showed up at harvest time to collect 75 percent of all the crops grown in the area as a tax.

This meant that it was highly unlikely that even after the storm had passed that there would be any federal agents in the area for some time. They just didn't have the manpower available to constantly monitor all the rural areas in Louisiana. He told his cousin that he would end the party and tell everyone what was going on. He would send Johnny back to the fishing boat with Ray, and he would guide the boat to an abandoned repair facility very close to the plantation. It was a covered wharf where the boat could be hidden from prying eyes.

They would be met there by the militia members with pickup trucks to offload all the supplies and hide them with all of Ray's men at secure locations. Then tomorrow they would discuss the ways they could help the fugitives get on the move to the place where they wanted to be. Ray knew that there would be much more to talk about later, but now they had to move, so he and his two men, along with Johnny headed back to the boat.

It took about forty-five minutes for the fishing boat to make the journey up the bayou to the covered repair facility, but that had been more than enough time for Daniel to bring in the militia members and their vehicles. Because the feds relied heavily on the produce, sugarcane, meat, and poultry produced by this rural community, they made sure that a limited but adequate supply of fuel was available for the farms, ranches, and plantations in the area. The Cajuns that ran these facilities had learned to ration the fuel carefully and hoard much of it. So they had fuel to move the trucks, food, ammunition, weapons, and men into hiding in a short period of time.

As Ray and his men disembarked from the boat, they were met by Daniel who Ray introduced to them. Then they found that they were in for a pleasant surprise. There were over fifty men, women, and even teenagers who were prepared to unload the boat and they would be able to do it quickly. Ray and the rest of his team did not need to be involved in this process; instead, they were treated to hot plates full of chicken and sausage gumbo, crawfish etouffee, and jambalaya that had been brought from the Cajun party to the landing site. For the fugitives, this was the best meal they had had in years.

The unloading of the fishing boat was completed shortly after three o'clock in the morning, and Ray and his team were taken to a large barn on the plantation where they were provided with bedding that would allow them to sleep comfortably on the ground for the rest of the night. Daniels's men would provide security overnight so all the fugitives could rest. There they could get a few hours of much-needed sleep and then prepare to proceed with the next part of the escape plan.

CHAPTER XIV

As instructed by Ray, Daniel awoke him and his men just after dawn, and the men were taken to the plantation home where they were provided with more luxuries that they had not enjoyed in years. It was a hot breakfast of scrambled eggs, Cajun boudin sausage, grits, homemade biscuits, and, most importantly, real coffee. After enjoying breakfast, Ray and Daniel sat down to talk business. The young man described the situation in the parish as being semi-stable. There were very few regular patrols in the area because the feds were still concentrating on controlling the large cities.

As a result, there had not been any effort made yet to go door to door and search for firearms. There had been an order issued for all privately owned firearms to be turned in to local authorities such as the sheriff, and he had reported to the feds that many had been received and destroyed. He did not report that most of them were small-caliber older weapons and that many of them were broken and worthless. Thus, the Donaldsonville militia was well armed and prepared to fight with other area militias when the time came, and they knew it would eventually happen.

Unfortunately, Ray had to inform Daniel that the time could be coming sooner rather than later. The night before, as they were pulling the *Freedom Runner* away from the wharf in New Orleans, there was a lot of lightning that illuminated the entire area and across the river on the west bank. Ray saw long lines of Russian- and Chinese-made tanks and other armored vehicles parked near a group of abandoned warehouses.

That confirmed something that Ray had overheard in the detention center dining area for the guards and administrators. They had invited some Syrian officers to eat dinner with them so they could impress them with Ray's cuisine. They were newly arrived and were commanders of a tank brigade that had recently arrived in New Orleans. Since they had no idea that Ray understood everything they were saying, they talked freely. Ray made a point of serving them personally but was careful not to be obvious. He did not hear the whole conversation but heard enough to know that they were the first element of a large force that was to assist the federal government in attacking a powerful rebel force in East Texas.

However, before they moved into that state, they had the task of finding and destroying some Louisiana National Guard units that it was suspected were hidden in the Donaldsonville area. The federal commanders were waiting on several Syrian infantry brigades and supporting artillery to arrive in the next three weeks. Ray felt he had no choice but to ask Daniel if he knew anything about such guard units in the area. Daniel hesitated momentarily then informed Ray that he did know about them and that he and Ray needed to immediately meet with the lieutenant colonel who commanded the units and who lived in the area.

They met Lieutenant Colonel Roger Griffin, a short wry middle-aged man, in the abandoned restaurant where the militia had been partying the night before. Daniel was the only person in the area who knew about the hidden guard units, and he assured the colonel that Ray could be trusted, and he had Ray tell him what he knew about the combined federal and Syrian operation. Ray also told the colonel and Daniel that he and his men were planning to head to East Texas where they had heard there was a strong resistance movement with a proactive commander that was recruiting more members for his growing militia.

Ray felt obligated to send some of his men immediately to Texas to alert the militia leaders that they were the ultimate target of this invasion. On the other hand, he and some of the other men would stay behind to help defend Daniel and the people of the Donaldsonville area if the colonel and Daniel thought they could be of assistance.

The colonel did not hesitate to be completely honest with Ray. There were elements of four different National Guard units hidden in the area and now were under his command. His own unit was an infantry battalion and the companies were scattered across south central Louisiana. The battalion headquarters had been in Donaldsonville but was now on an abandoned sugar plantation west of the city. The headquarters contingent was small consisting of the colonel, his executive officer, the battalion sergeant major, two other noncommissioned officers, and sixteen other infantrymen who were providing security. They were housed in the plantation house and surrounding buildings with their families.

The rest of the members of the headquarters company and the infantry battalion were still living with their families in Donaldsonville and other area towns and cities. They could be called up if necessary, but the battalion was woefully understrength. The federal government had cut the military drastically over the years including not only active-duty units but also reserve and National Guard units. After the EMP attack, the government had attempted to federalize the National Guard units.

In many states, the governors adamantly refused to allow this and deployed the National Guard units to assist people in their states, not to arrest them because they owned guns. When the federal government started to use the resources of the government police agencies and foreign troops in these states, many of the National Guard and reserve units took whatever equipment they could into hiding. That is what had happened in Louisiana, and so in addition to Colonel Griffin's infantry, there were also several other units hidden in the area. This included an armored battalion with six Abrams battle tanks, a Blackhawk helicopter unit with four Blackhawks, an Apache helicopter unit with five Apache attack choppers, and an MP unit with several Striker assault vehicles and some Humvees.

Griffin told Ray that there was no way his limited capabilities could successfully resist an assault by the forces that Ray had described. The addition of Ray and his men to his command would make no difference, and Daniel's militia would not be able to turn the tide either. This was particularly true since other Louisiana Guard units that had been in hiding in north Louisiana had been discovered and in most cases destroyed by federal troops and foreign mercenaries that had come in from Arkansas.

The colonel felt that it was time for the units under his command to withdraw and also go to Texas to join the forces there. He also wanted Daniel and his militia to come with them. His plan was relatively simple: he would supply Ray and his team with three Humvees driven by Texas guard members to convey them and as many of the weapons as they could carry to the Texas border. He wanted Ray to convey to the East Texas militia commander the readiness of Colonel Griffin to move his large National Guard force and area militia into Texas to join the Texas force.

The big question was, could the Texas group accommodate several hundred members of the Louisiana National Guard, militia members, and their families? They could bring tents for housing some of their people and some food, but they would have to have support from their counterparts in Texas. At this point, Daniel intervened and added his own thoughts to the discussion. He had always assumed that if things got really bad in the parish and his militia had to actively fight the feds that they would be supported by the National Guard. However, he realized that this was no longer possible.

Yet he was not ready to abandon the family plantation or the parish, and he felt that the other members of the militia would feel the same way. They would stay, but when the guard units moved out, Daniel and his family would go into temporary hiding. Since he was the only person that knew about their existence, he would not be available to answer any questions about them. Ray was not comfortable with that decision but knew that if were in Daniel's shoes, he would probably feel the same way.

It took the three men less than an hour to come up with a plan. Colonel Griffin would still supply Ray's team with the three Humvees and drivers to take them to the Texas border. They would also take all the weapons, ammo, and explosives they could carry. Once contact was made with the Texas militia commander and he hopefully agreed for the Louisiana guard units and their family members to join his militia, the Humvees and drivers would return to Donaldsonville, and the armor and infantry would move out for Texas.

The helicopters would also be sent into Texas but would initially stay on the border in case they were needed to provide air support for the ground units if they ran into trouble. The guard units would also bring half of the remaining armaments the escaped detainees had liberated in New Orleans. The other half would be hidden by Daniel so they would be used by his militia to strengthen its ability to defend their home parish.

CHAPTER XV

Just after dark that night, the Humvees and their passengers moved out. They would travel only at night without lights but using their night-vision equipment to navigate. It would still be slow going with one of the Humvees a half mile ahead on point. The route involved using small rarely traveled parish and country roads. The drivers of the Humvees had done a recon of the route several months earlier since Colonel Griffin wanted an escape route for his units if that became necessary. He was aware of the strong militia in Texas, so the route was specifically designed to get there safely to the Texas border that was controlled by the East Texas militia.

The recon had gone as far as the Sabine River that was near the town of Mansfield, Louisiana, just across the border from Texas. That would be a problem since they would have to cross the river to get into Texas. The East Texas militia controlled the west bank of the river, but federal troops had a guard post on the east side of the river. Ray's team would have to break through that post, but first, they had to get there.

At the rate they were able to travel at night, it would take three days to reach the bridge. The first forty-eight hours went smoothly with the vehicles making good time at night and hiding out in the thick western Louisiana wooded areas during the day. The locals in the area had little fuel for vehicles, so they only moved during the day and there were no encounters with other people. During the layovers, Jamie finally got a chance to get to know the other four inmates that were part of Ray's team. They had been housed in another barracks in the detention center so had not been a part of the meetings Jamie had attended.

There was a short but stout middle-aged man from Baton Rouge, Louisiana, named Juan Gonzales. His grandparents had legally emigrated from Mexico in the 1960s and become naturalized citizens. Thus, Juan's parents and he and his two brothers and his sister were all born American citizens. Juan was named after his grandfather who had worked for a landscaper in Baton Rouge and had eventually started his own very successful business.

His son Jorge had been working for the business part-time and was attending LSU, majoring in engineering, and a member of the air force ROTC unit. He graduated in 1968 and was commissioned a second lieutenant in the air force. He successfully completed flight school and was soon flying an F-4 Phantom fighter jet. His jet was shot down over North Vietnam, and he was killed in March 1971. His son Juan was only three years old at the time, so he didn't really remember his father but learned of his legacy from his mother and grandparents.

He grew up determined to follow in his father's footsteps. He graduated from LSU and received his commission in the air force and became a highly successful F-16 fighter pilot flying numerous combat missions during the never-ending war on terror. He had advanced in rank to be a lieutenant colonel in the air force but ended up in the detention center when he had refused a direct order to spy on his commanding general who was suspected by the new federal government of not being completely loyal to the new order.

Another member of the team was a young handsome former Louisiana State Police officer from Shreveport, Louisiana. His name was Samuel Bennett. He had grown up in family of several generations of police officers. He had gotten a degree from LSU in Shreveport in criminal justice and joined the state police. He was trained as a SWAT member and had soon advanced to being a team commander. His entire team was considered a danger to the federal control of the state of Louisiana, and they had been arrested along with members of other SWAT units around the state.

He did not know what had happened to the other men in his unit. Both Sam and Juan had wives and children, and they did not know their status but hoped to eventually be reunited with them. The other two men that Ray had recruited were from Texas and had been in the East Texas militia when they had been captured while on a recon patrol in western Louisiana. The first man was Gordon Travis, a direct descendant of Colonel William Travis who had been commander of the Alamo during the historic battle in 1836. He was a tall handsome blond young man who looked like he belonged in the movies. He had been born and raised in the small town of Van in Van Zandt County, Texas. He had gone to law school at the University of Texas and returned home to take over his father's practice in Van. He was also a captain in the Texas National Guard and had commanded an infantry company that had become part of the East Texas militia after the EMP attack.

The other Texan was Jack Jameson, a former firefighter in Dallas, Texas, who had been cited for heroism when he went into a burning house to rescue two small children. He had taken his oxygen mask off to provide them with the ability to breathe while he carried them out and had suffered some damage to his own lungs. The damage was severe enough so that he could no longer be an active firefighter. Because of his record, he was transferred to a prestigious position in headquarters but quickly became bored sitting behind a desk.

After talking to his wife, Jack decided to apply to be a police officer in his hometown of Canton, Texas. He was accepted, and they moved to Canton. A few months later, the EMP attack occurred, and everything changed. The East Texas militia was formed, and Jack volunteered to be a member. Both Travis and Jameson had been captured during a failed raid on federal forces. The militia had received intelligence reports that there was an ammunition dump in northwest Louisiana just across the border. The compound was just guarded by a platoon of federal troops and seemed to be a relatively soft target, but unfortunately, it had been reinforced by three other federal platoons just before the militia attack.

Travis and Jameson had only two platoons to make the attack that occurred at night; and when they ran into the larger federal force, they quickly realized they were outgunned, because not only were there more federal troops than militia soldiers, the feds had two heavy machine guns. Travis, who was in command of the operation, saw four of his men shot down by the unrelenting machine gun fire. He knew immediately that the attack would not be successful, so he ordered a withdrawal. He and one of the platoon sergeants, Jack Jameson, and two other troopers would hang back to provide covering fire for the retreat.

The plan was only partially successful, because while the militia teams were able to withdraw, two RPGs fired by federal troops hit the positions occupied by Travis, Jameson, and the other two soldiers before they could escape. Travis and Jameson were knocked unconscious by the RPG explosions, and the other two militia members were killed. When Travis and Jameson regained consciousness, they were both handcuffed to beds in a federal hospital in Shreveport, Louisiana. Their wounds were not life threatening, and they recovered quickly but did not consider this a blessing because they knew that the feds would soon be brutally interrogating both of them to get information about the location and strength of the East Texas militia.

However, that never happened because, either by accident or perhaps design by a sympathetic member of the hospital staff, the two men were not sent to the federal prison where they would be interrogated but instead sent to the New Orleans detention center where they were designated as political prisoners suitable for reeducation instead of captured members of the militia. There was no paper trail, so the federal commander in Shreveport never knew what happened to his prisoners.

Jamie talked for a while with these two men because he knew that they had provided Ray with the information about the East Texas militia that had led him to the conclusion that this was where he needed to take his men. Jamie learned that this militia was different from most of the local city and county militias that were set up for defense only. The general selected to command the Canton City militia had insisted that the militia be countywide. He had also insisted that the militia not be the government of the county. He would not command a military dictatorship. The county government and the town governments in the county would remain intact. The militia would be the military wing of those governments.

The general also wanted to have everyone in the county be in the militia. They would be trained in small unit tactics so they could not jut defend the county but be proactive, conducting recon patrols to track the movements of the federal troops and, in some cases, combat patrols to acquire weapons and other supplies from the enemy and kill as many of them as possible. His plan was successful, and soon many other counties placed their militias under his command. Within a year, twenty-six counties had become part of the East Texas militia. It had become a powerful force and one that had also become a grave concern to the federal government.

Jamie was intrigued and asked the two Texans who this general was. They said his name was Ben Donnelly. Jamie was stunned by the information but not really surprised. He knew immediately that the commander of the East Texas militia was his father.

CHAPTER XVI

Jamie immediately went to see Ray with this information because he was afraid it might endanger the whole escape plan.

"My dad probably considers me a traitor," Jamie told Ray. "If I am with you, he may refuse to accept you and the rest of the team into his territory. I can't be responsible for that. I need to go off on my own before we get to Texas."

Ray's response was adamant. "You are not leaving this unit, and you will let me deal with your father. Once he hears about whom you are now and how important you were to our escape, he will come around. Now get some sleep. We will be moving out in a few hours. That's an order."

Jamie did as he was ordered, but he didn't get much sleep. At a little after 4:00 p.m., the men in Ray's team were awakened by gunfire not far from where they were camped. All the men grabbed their weapons and set up a defensive perimeter around the wooded area where they were hiding their vehicles. Once that was accomplished, Ray took Bill Jackson and John Magee with him to find out what was going on. He left George Carson in charge of the rest of the men.

He and his small patrol moved out through the woods toward the continuing sounds of gunfire. It took only a few minutes for the team to reach the scene that was right along the road. Ray quickly saw that what was happening was a firefight between a federal patrol in four vehicles and a group of men who had clearly ambushed the patrol and bitten off more than they could chew. Ray saw eight men in the woods that were probably members of a local militia group, and they were in a fight with seventeen federal soldiers.

Ray was able to see that two federal soldiers were down, either dead or wounded, and three of the attackers were also down. Both sides had suffered casualties, but the federal force clearly had the advantage. They had automatic weapons that produced a much higher volume of fire than the semi-automatic used by the attackers.

This put Ray and his men in a quandary. He could not understand why the dwindling attack force had not just moved back into the thick woods where they might have been able to escape. However, it didn't really matter as Ray considered all the possibilities. First, he did not know if the attacking force was a patriot militia of just some outlaws trying to capture federal vehicles and weapons and ammunition. He also did not know if the federal unit had been able to contact other federal units in the area to come to their assistance. Either way, if the firefight continued or if additional federal forces arrived to end it, Ray and his team would lose access to the highway they needed to get into Texas.

Ray decided that his only option was to use his people to destroy the federal troops and open the road to Texas. He sent Captain Jackson back to bring up the rest of the team with the exception of the three National Guard drivers. If things went badly and they had to get back to the Humvees, he wanted the drivers ready to go. He also had Jamie stay with the vehicles because he was the only one in the team who did not have a background in either the military or police work. Ray would not put the boy at risk.

Ray and Magee moved away from the ambush site and met the rest of the men where they could cross the road unseen and get behind the federal forces. It just took a few minutes to move through the thick woods and get into position. Once they were in a place that gave them clear lines of sight on the enemy, Ray signaled them to open fire. Seven of the federal soldiers were dropped immediately. The other eight turned and got off a few ineffective shots at Ray's men before they were also cut down.

Ray and his men cautiously approached the federal position but made sure the vehicles on the road shielded them from the other group of fighters because Ray was still not sure who they were. As they checked the feds and found that they were all dead, Ray heard someone thanking him and his men for saving them. Ray saw that one of the men had stepped out onto the road with his weapon raised above his head. Ray stepped out to meet him and found that his name was John Turner and he was the commander of a group that was actually the remnants of a Louisiana National Guard infantry company.

They were one of about a dozen units in north Louisiana that had gone into hiding after the EMP attack when the feds tried to turn National Guard units into an arm of the new federal government. They had taken their families with them and managed to survive until a few months ago when federal forces had launched a major offensive in north Louisiana to hunt down the units. Turner believed it was because the government was concerned about the hidden units making their way to East Texas to join up with the militia there.

In fact, Turner told Ray that had been the plan when the federal sweep started. They had to have been tipped off by someone inside the units because they moved swiftly and decisively against the guard units and destroyed them. They were merciless, killing most of the guard members and some of their families. The rest they sent to detention centers to be reeducated.

Turner's unit had been alerted by two men that had escaped from a tank unit that had been attacked. However, the warning came too late. Before Captain Turner was able to get his unit organized to move out, they got hit; but since they knew an attack was imminent, the company put up a hell of a fight. They inflicted heavy casualties on the enemy but suffered heavy casualties of their own. Turner was ultimately able to escape with twenty-two men and most of the women and children. They were now hidden several miles away, but they had little food, and so Turner had taken some of his men to the highway in the hope of ambushing a federal convoy and getting food and some ammunition and weapons that they also needed. Then they planned on trying to make it to Texas.

The plan was to kill the federal troops in their convoy, steal their uniforms, and use them to disguise members of the militia. They would drive the vehicles and use their cover to attack the men guarding the west side of the bridge. Then they could cross into Texas. Ray saw this as an opportunity to breach the federal defense at the bridge for both the Louisiana guard unit and his team.

The problem was that Turner had told Ray that the federal unit they had attacked was actually the relief guard force for the troops guarding the bridge. That means they were scheduled to be at the bridge in a few hours. With the delay caused by the extended firefight on the road, it was going to be impossible for him to bring the rest of his unit and their families forward and make it to the bridge on time for the changing of the guard. Being a few minutes late would probably not be a problem, but under current circumstances, they would arrive at least an hour late. This could cause the bridge guards to be on high alert and possibly have contacted other federal units to come to their support.

Ray had to come to a quick decision because he only had two choices: have Turner and his guardsmen conduct the ruse with Ray's men in support or have his team take the identities of the federal troops and have Turner and his people follow in the three Humvees. He chose the latter option and had his men don the uniforms of the dead federal troops. However, of his thirteen men, he only put eight in the false identities. The other five men were assigned to get out of the vehicles and approach the bridge area through the surrounding woods and prepare to provide covering fire for the undercover unit.

CHAPTER XVII

The plan unfolded as it was designed. The convoy containing the disguised men approached the checkpoint that consisted of a retractable steel gate covered by two manned sandbagged positions at each end of the gate. Behind the gate was an aluminum building that served as the guardhouse where the guards would go to get some rest or eat their MREs. Ray had sent a patrol out ahead of the vehicles to check out the defenses.

They saw ten federal guards in the area, but it was a very relaxed atmosphere with most of the guards lounging around with their weapons leaning against sandbags instead of in their hands. There were only two of them actually on alert at the gate. They were obviously not expecting any trouble. In fact, they seemed more interested in keeping an eye on the Texas side of the Sabine River instead of the Louisiana side.

The patrol was being led by George Carson, accompanied by Tim Johnson, Juan Gonzales, Sam Bennett, and Jamie. Jamie had no formal military training, but his father had taught him to shoot and to move quietly through the woods. He had begged Ray to allow him to participate in this operation, and Ray had reluctantly agreed. Jamie had been a part of the team that had escaped, so Ray believed he was entitled to be a part of this.

After their recon, George reported to Ray, and the plan was put into operation. The three Humvees that were captured from the federal forces were standard issue, but one of them was equipped with a top-mounted M2 machine gun. That had been the lead vehicle in the federal convoy, and that would be the case when they approached the federal guard post.

It was just after dark when Ray's disguised team pulled up toward the gate. The guards had the area well lighted since the river was fairly narrow at this point, and people could try to swim across instead of using the bridge. This lighting set the guards up clearly for George Carson's team that had moved into the nearby woods. When the fake convoy approached the guard post, the guards were all outside waiting to be relieved, and George's team opened up first, quickly taking out several guards. At the same time, Magee opened up with the M2, and Ray's team poured out of the Humvees. The combined firepower of Ray and his men disguised as federal troops and the patrol killed the remaining guards in a matter of seconds.

Ray then ordered two of the three Humvees to be driven back down the road to bring up the Louisiana National Guard unit survivors. Since there were a total of fifty-four people, the children were loaded in the three Humvees that Ray's team had originally used, but the rest of the men and women had to walk, so the progression had been slow. Now at least, the rest could ride in either the additional vehicles or on top and could get to the river faster.

However, before they arrived, Ray had to make contact with the East Texas militia across the river. He knew that they would not just allow anyone into the counties they controlled. They did not want to turn away refugees, but because of limited resources such as food and housing, they had no choice. They were only allowing families into the area if they were related to the people in the counties, had a family member with a military or first-responder background, were other members of the medical profession, or had other special skills that could benefit the militia.

Ray knew that everyone with him fell into those categories; but he had to convince the Texas militia leaders of that fact and also to get them to accept the fact that many more families would be arriving with the helicopter, infantry, and armor units that were to follow. While he thought about all this, Ray was also carefully watching the west side of the river across the Sabine River Bridge. He didn't see anybody, but he knew the members of the Texas militia were there somewhere because they had to have heard the gunfire and sent out a patrol to investigate.

Ray knew they were probably suspicious since he and some of his men were still wearing the federal uniforms. He felt that changing out of the uniforms with the militia watching would just increase their suspicion. He decided to make his move before the National Guard members and families showed up. He laid down his M16 rifle and removed his belt and holster that contained his Glock 19 pistol. He then raised his hands and began moving through the bridge lights toward the west end of the bridge. He had ordered his men to stand down, so there were no weapons being pointed toward the west side, although the men had their weapons at the ready.

When Ray reached the end of the bridge, he still saw no movement ahead of him, so he yelled out to the darkness, "I am Lieutenant Colonel Raymond Thibodeaux, formerly of the US Army Special Forces. I have recently escaped from a federal detention center in New Orleans with other former inmates that are with me. We also have some survivors of the Louisiana National Guard and their families coming up behind us. We want to join up with the Texas militia."

For a few moments, there was no response, and Ray was wondering if he had been mistaken and no one was out there. Then someone in the darkness responded to him, and he immediately recognized the voice of the man that said, "Hell, Colonel, aren't you way too old for this type of crap?"

Ray breathed a sigh of relief, lowered his hands, and answered the inquiry, "Is that really you, Sergeant McElroy? I can't believe the Texas militia is so desperate that they would accept a lowlife SOB like you." Ray heard a chuckle as the former first sergeant of his Green Beret Company, Greg McElroy, emerged from the darkness. They shook hands and embraced, and Ray saw that his friend and former senior noncommissioned officer of the company he had commanded now wore the insignia of a major in the East Texas militia. McElroy was a handsome redheaded Irishman with a quick temper and outspoken nature that did not endear him to others. However, he was a great soldier, and he and Ray had quickly bonded when they served together and become a successful team. This was the first time they had seen each other in many years.

They were glad to reunite, but both knew that this was not the time or place to swap war stories and reconnect. Ray told McElroy about his team's escape and how they had stumbled into the fight between the federal relief convoy and the members of the Louisiana National Guard. He said that the National Guard group should at the bridge within an hour. He also wanted to know if they would all be allowed to join the Texas force.

McElroy said that was not his call. The commanding general would have to decide that, but in the meantime, they had to prepare themselves to defend against a possible incursion by federal troops. McElroy explained that the enemy rotated their guards at the bridge once a week. He believed that the main base where the guards came from was only a few hours away. When the relieved unit did not show up, the feds would assume something was wrong and send out a heavily armed patrol to find out what had happened.

The major also explained that he was in charge of all the militia guard posts along the Sabine River that formed much of the eastern border of the counties controlled by the militia. He just happened to be checking on this particular post tonight when they heard the firing break out. Each guard post had one squad of eight men assigned to it, and there were platoon-strength reinforcements scattered along the areas behind the border. They were each assigned to move to one of four posts if necessary. The one assigned to this particular post had been immediately alerted by McElroy and was on its way, but it might take as long as ninety minutes to get there.

The commanding general had also been alerted, and two special operations teams had been dispatched from his headquarters in Canton, Texas. However, they were also several hours away; and unfortunately, McElroy had no way of knowing how quickly a reactive federal force would arrive. He told Ray that as soon as the National Guard unit came in with their families, Ray's team would join with the soldiers of the Texas militia and the guardsmen to establish a defense perimeter while the families were moved to the rear.

The major was worried because he did not know how the feds would react when they discovered that their guard detachment had been wiped out and he did not know how large the federal force would be. They might decide to immediately launch an assault into Texas or wait for further reinforcements, but the militia could not take any chances. They had to prepare to defend against an all-out attack.

The concern was legitimate since the federal forces arrived at the bridge just thirty minutes after the Louisiana National Guard unit and families had moved across it. The families were packed into two of the Humvees recently occupied by Ray's team, plus the three liberated federal Humvees. Two of the Humvees had a mounted machine gun and would have to be part of the bridge's defense. The other vehicles would take the families to a rear position while some of the National Guard troops were deployed to defend them.

Ray and his former first sergeant were close enough to the bridge to see the federal unit approach it. The force appeared to be about forty men, which made it approximately platoon strength. That meant that when it came to manpower, the patriot strength was equal to that of the federal troops. The feds had three armored Humvees and two large troop transport trucks. What was most worrisome to McElroy was that they also had a Stryker assault vehicle that was a heavily armored infantry transport unit mounted with a remote-controlled 50-caliber machine gun.

That was heavier than anything that the militia had, and the standard grenade launchers they had were not capable of penetrating the Stryker armor. They could not destroy it or even slow it down. If it was used to lead a federal attack across the bridge, the militia would be basically defenseless. Then Ray told McElroy that this was not necessarily the case. Among the items seized from the hidden location in New Orleans were several RPGs and some C-4 explosives. Ray told McElroy his plan, and the major readily agreed.

CHAPTER XVIII

Ray got two of his men to grab some RPGs and C-4 from the Humvees. As a Green Beret, John Magee had been trained in several specialties, and one of them was disarming improvised explosive devices (IEDs). That specialty meant that he could also create and deploy IEDs, but there was not much time. Ray and McElroy had seen a heated discussion going on near the bridge between two federal officers. Obviously, nothing could be heard of the conversation, but one of the officers was pointing across the river toward the militia position. He clearly wanted to attack across the bridge, and by the time Magee had retrieved the explosives, the feds were preparing to move.

They lined up to cross the bridge, and as expected, the Stryker was in the lead with the Humvees following and the infantry behind them. They were moving slowly because they had no idea what the strength of the Texas militia was. This allowed Magee to quickly rig several IEDs alongside the road where the militia roadblock and guard post were set up. It was similar to the federal position in that there was a small guardhouse and two bunkers to allow the men to have secure firing positions. When the feds reached the militia guard post, they would find it abandoned, but lights would be left on so the militia could see the attackers while hiding in the dark woods themselves.

McElroy had deployed Ray and his men in the thick woods to the right of the guard post and his militia on the left side. The Louisiana National Guard unit was deployed farther down the road from the guard post as a blocking force to prevent the feds from getting past them to their families. They were also prepared to move forward to support the militia if necessary.

Magee and his men had hidden the hastily rigged IEDs in weeds on the side of the road, but they did not have the time or equipment to set up remote detonations by radio. Instead, they used the command wire devices that had been seized with the C-4. This allowed them to run a cable from the IEDs into the thick woods so they could detonate the devices from a safe and covered position. The heavy armor of the Stryker made it immune from anything but multiple RPG strikes, but the wheels were vulnerable to an IED explosion, and RPGs could then be used to knock out the turret that housed the remotely fired 50-caliber machine gun.

In a few minutes, the entire federal column had moved across the bridge and the Stryker remained on the point. As it approached the IEDs, Magee was watching closely and set off the explosives at just the right time. The wheels of the Stryker were seriously damaged, and the vehicle came to a halt. At the same moment, two other members of Ray's team fired RPGs at the Stryker and took out the machine gun. Then the rest of the militia and Ray's team opened fire on the two Humvees and the supporting infantry. They were laying down heavy fire, but the federal troops were also replying with heavy fire, and the one Humvee with a machine gun was spraying the woods. The feds could not see the men shooting at them, but they could see the muzzle flashes from their weapons, so the militia and Ray's men were taking casualties.

The tide turned quickly in favor of the militia when an RPG took out the Humvee with the machine gun. The intense fire had also killed the federal officer who had ordered the attack, and the remaining officer signaled his men to withdraw along with the last Humvee that could not go forward in any case with the two disabled vehicles blocking the road. With the Louisiana Guard members not directly involved in the fight, the feds outnumbered the militia and Ray's men, but the federal officer knew that he was facing highly trained troops. He also knew that his own men were mostly new recruits who had received minimal training and were not really prepared for a sustained firefight.

That was the problem for federal forces all around the county. Very few American military veterans had gone over to the new federal government that had abolished the Constitution that the veterans had sworn to defend. That meant that the feds had to get its fighters from the dwindling number of true believers in the progressive cause. The other recruits were brought in by using a combination of material inducements such as more food for their families or by essentially being drafted and threatened with imprisonment or death if they refused to serve. This did not make for a reliable military, and that was the reason that the strong force built up in New Orleans consisted mostly of foreign fighters, many from Middle Eastern countries.

The surviving federal officer realized he was in a fight he could not win, so he decided to cut his losses and retreat back across the river to wait for reinforcements. However, before they arrived, the relief militia platoon came in to join McElroy's men and was soon followed by the two special operation teams dispatched from Canton. This meant that even when a platoon of federal reinforcements arrived at the river, they would be outnumbered by the augmented militia force.

The lieutenant in command of the relief federal platoon had been ordered by his superiors not to move across the river and was appalled that the now-deceased commander of the platoon that had arrived before him had made such an attack. The lieutenant had just been ordered to reestablish and reinforce the river guard post and do nothing else. This was because of the fact, unknown to the lieutenant, that the large column of tanks, artillery, and infantry being assembled in New Orleans would be ready to move out within a week.

It was now dawn on the Sabine River, and McElroy had received reports form his scouts that while the feds were reinforcing their guard post, there were no indications that they were going to try to cross the bridge into Texas territory again. This was good news for Ray and his former first sergeant because it meant they had won a decisive victory. However, it had not come without a price. Two members of the militia had been killed and three others wounded. Ray's team had also taken a hit. Jason Arnaud, the coast guard veteran who had guided them up the river, had been killed by machine gun fire from a federal Humvee, and Tim Johnson, one of Magee's men who had helped the team escape, had been badly wounded when a hand grenade thrown by a federal soldier had exploded near him. Tim and the other wounded were treated by the medic that was with the Louisiana National Guard and then transported by Humvee to the nearest medical center in Longview, Texas.

Fourteen of the enemy had been killed and six more wounded. McElroy sent an envoy across the river with a white flag and had him tell the federal commander that he could come collect his wounded and dead. This was done, and the men on both sides of the river settled into an uneasy temporary truce. Neither commander knew what the other side might do, so both sides were setting up defensive positions on their side of the river. Ray and his men did what they could to help but had McElroy send a message to the commanding general to let him know what Ray and the Louisiana National Guard had to offer to the East Texas militia. Ray also had McElroy inform the general that he had some important intelligence info for him and that his son Jamie was one of the inmates that had escaped with the team.

CHAPTER XIX

Ray soon learned from McElroy that the general was already on his way with a full company of reinforcements. He wanted to check out the situation at the border crossing himself. Ray had heard this was usually the case with General Donnelly; while he trusted his commanders in the field, he was hesitant about making some decisions that would send his troops into harm's way without personally making an assessment.

Donnelly had become a legend among the resistance in Texas and the surrounding states because they had nothing but respect for his leadership and what he had accomplished. He and his wife had been relative newcomers to the Canton, Texas, area when the EMP attack had occurred. Chaos had reigned for several weeks with residents emptying the shelves of local stores and the Van Zandt County and local city government trying to continue to provide basic services to their citizens and also prepare what they knew might be a major influx of refugees from Dallas.

The city and county leaders also knew that they would need organized defensive help, so they decided to form city and county militias. They went to the local VFW and American Legion posts to recruit their members to be the backbone of the militia and hopefully provide militia commanders. Ben Donnelly had become a member of the Canton VFW and quickly had gained the respect of the other members. As was the norm for veterans, they did not talk about their awards for heroism, but they would share war stories.

In Donnelly's case, one of the members of the VFW had served under his command during the war on terror and knew his history. Donnelly had been an infantry battalion commander and had served several tours in Iraq and Afghanistan. During that time, he had distinguished himself both for his tactical expertise and his devotion to his men. He had earned two Silver Stars, a Bronze Star, and a Purple Heart. He was always on the front during battles, personally leading his men.

Donnelly had written a best-selling book about his experiences that focused not on himself but on the bravery of his men. This further endeared him to the members of the VFW post. As a result, when the VFW members were approached by the civil authorities and asked to recommend a county militia commander, they were solidly in favor of Donnelly. Their recommendation was accepted, and Ben Donnelly was asked to present a plan to the county for a militia. However, what he came up with was not just a plan for the militia but a plan for the entire county and, eventually, surrounding counties. He first insisted that the militia would only serve as the military component of the county. The city and county governments would remain intact with elections conducted as usual. He did not want to subvert the Constitution by establishing a military dictatorship.

Cities and towns such as Canton would still provide police and firefighters for their communities, and the reminder of the county would be under the jurisdiction of the county sheriff and his deputies. The militia would only step in during extraordinary circumstances. It would be up to the towns and the county to set up a way to compensate these men and women for their services. The militia's primary job would be to protect the border of the county from incursions either by looters or by federal forces. In order to do that, Donnelly wanted to make sure that his soldiers were highly trained and not just a ragtag group of men with weapons.

There were many military veterans in Van Zandt County, and it had also become a retirement destination for many police and firefighters from the Dallas area, so there was a lot of talent to be tapped into. Veterans in the community were so highly prized that this small Texas town had established a beautiful veterans memorial that was visited by thousands of people each year. The situation that America faced was similar to that prior to and during the Revolutionary War. At that time, all male members of the communities were required to be in the militia. The general proposed the same system for the county. In fact, everyone in the county between the ages of eighteen and sixty-five would be required to serve in some capacity based on their physical abilities.

The military veterans received assignments based on their ranks and military skill sets. There were over three hundred veterans in the county, and it was estimated that there were enough able-bodied individuals in the county of over ten thousand citizens to create two full infantry battalions consisting of three companies each and a headquarters unit. Each battalion would have about eight hundred soldiers including officers and noncommissioned officers.

Half of the veterans would train the civilians in small arms weapons and tactics while the other half manned checkpoints blocking the entrances to the county. Fortunately, virtually every family in the county owned firearms of various types, and many had been stockpiling ammunition for several years until its availability was restricted by the government. So all members of the militia had to initially supply their own weapons and ammunition—and willingly did so. There was a wide variety of weapons from bolt-action hunting rifles to semi-automatic AK-47s and AR-15s along with many pistols and shotguns.

Ammunition was obviously precious, and since most residents were already good shots, there was no reason for most of them to engage in target practice. The obvious problem was that there were not any heavy weapons to speak of, although a few residents did admit to secretly owning some outlawed fully automatic weapons. The situation regarding ammunition and automatic weapons was partially solved by the family that owned a very large firearm dealership in the countryside outside of Canton. Their license-to-sell firearms had been revoked by the federal government even before the EMP attack. Federal agents had showed up at their business and home to inventory and seize their weapons and ammunition but found nothing. The owners Todd and Jane Buchanan and their two sons, Caleb and Chris, claimed that they had sold their remaining inventory to buyers from another county. Of course, they had no records of this sale.

The five federal police officers immediately arrested the Buchanan family in order to take them back to their headquarters in Dallas where they could be interrogated. However, when they emerged from the family home with their captors, they discovered they had a problem. There were over a hundred armed men surrounding the home and the two federal vehicles. No one said a word, but the intention of the men was clear. The feds would not be taking the Buchanan family anywhere. The federal police officers got the message and quickly got into their vehicles and drove away. This was the first encounter they had with the people of Van Zandt County, but it was only the beginning.

The next day a much larger contingent of the federal police showed up at the Buchanan home again, but the family was long gone. They had moved to their cabin deep in the East Texas woods, but they were not actually living there. They were in an underground bunker they had constructed on the fifteen-acre property a few years before. It was a large bunker with living and sleeping quarters for the family as well as a small kitchen. There was also a large pantry stocked with food and water that would keep the family alive for at least two years. The whole bunker had an electrical system run by carefully camouflaged solar panels.

In addition, there was a tunnel from the family bunker to another bunker where they had stored numerous weapons, ammunition, and large amounts of black powder. There was also a workroom with a big supply of parts needed to convert semi-automatic weapons to full automatic. After the EMP attack, Todd Buchanan heard that there were militia units being formed in Van Zandt County. He then found out that the newly appointed county militia commander had called for a meeting of all veterans in the county, and as a former officer of the elite marine recon units, Todd decided to attend.

He was impressed by what he heard, primarily because General Donnelly did not intend to have the militia be just a defensive force. He was going to organize his units and train them to not only defend the county and its towns but also to conduct both short- and long-range reconnaissance patrols so they could find out if any threats were developing in neighboring counties. In addition, he was going to have his units conduct combat patrols against targets of opportunity such as federal patrols, raiding parties, or just criminal gangs. Such raids could prevent attacks on the county and hopefully secure additional weapons, ammunition, and other supplies for the militia.

After the meeting, Todd approached the general and offered his services. He felt like he could best help by having him and his family be the armorers for the militia. They would convert certain weapons to fully automatic mode, reload ammunition, and even create homemade hand grenades and other explosives. He could also provide some additional weapons and ammo to the militia. General Donnelly readily agreed and appointed Todd as his armorer with the rank of major in the militia.

CHAPTER XX

When General Donnelly arrived at the border crossing, the first thing he wanted to do was see his son, but he was approached first by Ray who told him that his son was worried that his father would reject him as a traitor. Ray quickly explained to him that his son was a true patriot who had been arrested for trying to help the federal detainees in New Orleans. He also informed the general about his son's heroism in helping to initiate the escape of Ray and his team.

Ben Donnelly told Ray that he had never doubted that his son would eventually see the light and follow the right path. With that assurance, Ray took the general to the guard shack where he was able to see and embrace his son for the first time in many years. It was a bittersweet reunion, because while Jamie was grateful for his father accepting him back into the family, he was devastated to learn that while his bothers were still alive, his mother had died several years ago from cancer. Jamie knew that if he had not left his family, he could have been present to say good-bye to his mother. Ben could only reassure him that his mother had never stopped loving Jamie and always knew that Jamie loved her.

Their conversation had to be brief because the general had much to do, but Jamie had a request. He had spoken briefly with some of the members of one of the East Texas militia special operation units that had arrived earlier in the day. He told his father that he was ready and willing to go through whatever training was necessary for him to become a part of one of the units. Ben Donnelly had to smile as he looked at his scrawny son who had obviously suffered greatly while a captive of the federal regime. He nodded his head and told his Jamie that as his mother used to say, "We need to fatten you up first. Then I'll turn you over to the tough bastards who run our special operations training camp."

There were now eight special operations teams in the East Texas militia. The core personnel were veterans of the army rangers, Green Berets, Navy SEALs, marine recon, and air force commandos. They ran a rigorous training program for volunteers who wanted to join the elite force. The program had continued to expand in the years since the EMP attack as had the militia. Shortly after the Van Zandt County militia had been formed, General Donnelly had reached out to surrounding counties that were also forming militias or considering forming them.

He met with the leaders and told them that he believed the counties would be safer if they coordinated their efforts and provided mutual defensive and offensive capabilities. The wisdom of his plans was immediately seen by those he talked to, and the militia expanded into one county after another. While this was happening, the federal forces were also expanding, often with the help of foreign troops and mercenaries. The feds had initially been responsible for taking control of the major cities in Texas and around the nation. They handled the cities in Texas the same way that Jamie had seen it done New Orleans.

The feds' primary focus was not on protecting lives and property from looters and other criminals or providing basic services to the surviving residents but disarming the American citizens who were trying to protect themselves. For example, in Dallas, Texas, thousands of people had been killed while thousands more had fled the city. The feds basically allowed the criminal gangs to have their way in the city and actually brought them in as allies to help control the streets and the population. They also allied themselves with the Mexican drug cartels that were operating freely throughout Texas because of the open-border policy of the federal government.

However, controlling the cities was difficult because there were Americans who fought back, but they were not as well organized as the militias in East Texas had become. This chaos in the cities had bought the time the militia needed to train and be ready for the defense of East Texas. The feds did send patrols into counties surrounding the big cities, some of them heavily armed and supported by armored vehicles like Humvees and Strykers. The intention was to intimidate the populations and, if possible, disarm them. It not only didn't work, it became an epic failure.

Donnelly had ordered the militia trained for both defensive and offensive operations. When militia recon patrols discovered an intrusion by the feds into the counties they controlled, a militia combat unit was sent in. Sometimes it was a special operations unit or a combination of such units and regular militia troops. They were proving to be highly successful in ambushing the federal units, killing the federal soldiers, and seizing their vehicles, equipment, and supplies.

These actions not only soon discouraged the feds from further incursions but also provided the militia with much-needed heavy weapons and armored vehicles. The militia's strength was further augmented by the return of National Guard and reserve units to active duty in the counties. After the EMP attacks, the governor of Texas had sent many such units to secure the Texas borders in clear defiance of the orders by the federal government to put all those units under its control. The units in East Texas were covering the state's northeastern and eastern borders with Oklahoma, Arkansas, and Louisiana.

As the militia got stronger, its members were able to take over the border patrol from the overstretched National Guard and reserve units so that the soldiers could go home and spend some much-needed and long-overdue time with their families. Eventually, the guard and reserve units that were legally federal units but whose soldiers had revolted were merged into the militia and the commanders readily submitted to be commanded by General Donnelly. Some of the National Guard units were part of a military police brigade. These units were armed with regulation 9mm pistols, M4 carbines or M16 automatic rifles, and some heavier weapons such as machine guns and grenade launchers. They also had armored Humvees and some Stryker vehicles. Other different types of units had provided the militia with some light artillery, a dozen tanks, a variety of mortars, and machine guns.

CHAPTER XXI

The militia was now better armed but lacked any air power, antiaircraft capability, and heavy artillery. Thus, General Donnelly was delighted to learn from Ray that the Louisiana National Guard units coming from Donaldsonville would be providing his command with both Blackhawk and Apache helicopters, as well as some additional tanks. He knew that the federal government would eventually be forced to launch a major assault against his militia and the area they controlled that had now been dubbed the Alamo by the people in Texas and the surrounding states.

Therefore, the general was not surprised by the intelligence Ray had gathered about the enemy force being amassed in New Orleans that had East Texas as its ultimate target. He immediately had the Louisiana National Guard members who had transported Ray and his team to Texas return to Louisiana and bring the members of the units, their families, and their equipment into Texas. They could obviously not leave the way they had entered, but there was a pontoon bridge that had secretly been constructed across the Sabine River, south of the bridge where Ray and his team had crossed. It was well concealed and had been used by the Texas militia to send recon patrols into Louisiana.

The guard members moved carefully but made it back to their headquarters near Donaldsonville, Louisiana, within a few days; and forty-eight hours later, the ground units and their families had moved out. Several Humvees with well-armed troops were on the point, and the tanks followed them. The rest of the vehicles were right behind the tanks. There were some Strykers and numerous other vehicles including vans and military trucks that carried more troops, their families, and what meager possessions they were allowed to bring with them. The vehicles were also filled to the brim with weapons, fuel, and ammunition.

It had been planned to have the helicopter units remain in place initially so they could be called in to provide fire support in case the ground units ran into trouble. Fortunately, that did not happen; and once the ground units reported they were safely in Texas, the choppers took off, loaded with additional supplies and fuel. They landed at a small airport right outside of Canton, Texas, where they were soon joined by the ground units. The helicopters and military vehicles were dispersed to hidden locations in the area, and the families and troops were put up for the time being in a tent city hidden in the woods. They would eventually have more substantial housing built for them, but now the top priority was elsewhere.

Since Ray had informed General Donnelly of the impending attack coming up from New Orleans, all preparations had to be made to meet that attack and to deal with a buildup of federal forces that was occurring to the west along the border between Dallas County and Kaufman County. The feds controlled Dallas County that included the devastated city of Dallas and its suburbs while the East Texas militia controlled Kaufman County. The city of Mesquite that was right on the eastern county line had avoided most of the initial rioting and destruction that had occurred in the rest of the Dallas metropolitan area. Its small but effective city militia had turned away the looters but fell quickly when the feds attacked in force.

This particular force consisted of a small but heavily armed contingent of federal troops that had been augmented by an unholy alliance with various vicious gangs in the Dallas area. The federal agreement with the gangs was simple. They would be armed and assist in the attack on Mesquite. Their payment would be free rein to loot the homes and businesses in the city.

The attack came quickly and was unexpected, so the Kaufman County militia and the rest of the East Texas militia had not even been able to mobilize and react. The gang members ran wild and not only looted the city but raped women and girls and murdered many of the male inhabitants. The feds allowed this to happen for a few days and then offered the gangs the same opportunity to assist in the invasion of Kaufman County. The gangs agreed, and the feds began consolidating and building up their forces along the county border.

It was a formidable force consisting of two companies of federal troops containing over five hundred men as well as over a thousand gang members. They had RPGs, grenades, machine guns, and many other automatic weapons. They also said some armored Humvees and several Strykers. As they massed on the county border, the Kaufman militia dug in with strong defensive positions. General Donnelly responded by moving in a full battalion of militia infantry from Van Zandt County that was just to the east of Kaufman to support the defenders.

The East Texas militia had continued to grow over the years and now consisted of over ten thousand troops, so Donnelly knew that they could defeat the threat on their western border, but he was suspicious. There was something else going on here. He sent out several recon patrols that found what he had suspected: there was an Iranian army armored platoon with four tanks supported by two infantry companies in reserve about five miles behind the federal position on the Kaufman County border. This gave the feds a much stronger force, but it made Donnelly even more suspicious.

First, the feds must know that reconnaissance patrols were regularly conducted by the militia, yet no real effort had been made to conceal the Iranian reserve position. Secondly, even though the feds did not know the exact strength of the militia, they surely knew that it could probably be able to defend the border against the force that was currently being arrayed against it. The general's suspicions were confirmed by what Ray Thibodeaux had told him. The buildup on the border of Kaufman County was essentially a ruse to cause the major part of the militia to deploy against that threat. That would leave the Alamo vulnerable to the attack coming from the east.

The general decided that in order to deal with the pending attack from the east, his militia would have to first go on the offensive and eliminate the threat on the western border. However, he had no way of knowing how soon the attack from the east would materialize. He had discussed this with Ray when he had first been told about the enemy force in New Orleans and Ray had come up with a plan to slow the advance down. He sent word to his cousin Daniel with the National Guard members who were returning to Donaldsonville to lead their units to Texas. They informed Daniel that Ray wanted him to mobilize his local militia to do what they could to hinder the enemy movement through Louisiana. To help facilitate this effort, General Donnelly dispatched two East Texas Special Operations teams to assist Daniel's men.

CHAPTER XXII

By the time the East Texas militia units arrived, Daniel had heard that the force out of New Orleans was ready to move in a day or two. Daniel's militia was over three hundred strong and was now well armed thanks to Ray and the National Guard leaving it some automatic weapons, ammunition, hand grenades, and C-4 explosives. Since Daniel had no military experience, the actual commander of the militia was a thirty-four-year-old former marine recon first sergeant, who had been heavily involved in the war on terror for several years. The sergeant was Frank Hebert, a fit young Cajun who had once been a star running back on the Donaldsonville High School football team but had chosen to join the Marine Corps instead of playing football in college.

He and Daniel met with the two East Texas special forces leaders: Roger Hall, a former Navy SEAL, and Norman Blake, a former Green Beret. Both had been appointed to train and lead special forces teams made up of a combination of military veterans and young men who had undergone rigorous training to become elite fighters for freedom.

The four men had to devise a strategy for protecting the people of Donaldsonville while at the same time delaying the advance of the federal troops and doing as much damage to them as much as possible. However, they all agreed that before they could make any final plans they needed to know if the enemy was on the move and what its strength was. It was agreed that Norman Blake and his team would leave immediately to find out what was coming.

Within twenty-four hours, Blake's team was just north of New Orleans, and they had seen the federal troops moving out of the city and determined that it was indeed a major force. There were thirty-two tanks, twenty-four mobile artillery pieces, thirty Stryker vehicles, and at least two thousand infantry troops. However, they were moving slowly, stopping first in Laplace, Louisiana, to look for National Guard units in hiding. They searched for several days but found nothing because the units had already moved north. This gave Blake's team the time they needed to get back to Donaldsonville so that they could develop a strategy.

As the militia leaders and the special operations commanders met once again, they formulated a plan. For the most part, the people in the Donaldsonville area had not known that National Guard units were even in the area and obviously had not known where they were located. So the four men in charge could use this by creating a false narrative that would send the federal force to a false location, where at least part of the force could be trapped. Not far from the city was the Atchafalaya Swamp. It is the largest wetlands area in the United States, covering over 1.4 million acres.

There are many hunting and fishing camps on the edge of or on islands in the swamp, and several of them would be a suitable location for hiding National Guard units. One in particular was known to the men of the Donaldsonville militia. It was accessed on a single road that crossed two bridges over large bayous several miles away from the hunting camp that had not been used in a long time.

The plan was actually very simple and initially consisted of the East Texas special operations team under the command of Norman Blake taking a platoon of the Louisiana militia out to harass and slow down the advance of the federal column. By the time the militia force approached Laplace, Louisiana, the feds were heading up Airline Highway toward a bridge where they could cross the Mississippi River and use State Highway 70 to move into Donaldsonville. They would cross on the Sunshine Bridge, originally called the bridge to nowhere.

It had been built in 1964 under the administration of Governor Jimmy Davis who was a country singer and songwriter who had become famous for his iconic song "You Are My Sunshine." Thus, the bridge was named for the song and became a joke because the project was underfunded and initially went from Gonzales,

Louisiana, on the east bank of the river to a swamp on the west bank. After many years, it finally was connected to State Highway 70 and became an important hurricane evacuation route for residents of south Louisiana. Now, it had become the route for invaders.

The bridge was heavily guarded by federal troops, so the militia units crossed the Mississippi River upstream in small boats and deployed south of the Sunshine Bridge along Airline Highway. There were thick wooded areas along parts of the highway, so Blake divided his force into three teams made up members of his special operations unit and members of the Louisiana militia platoon. They were deployed in a staggered formation. Each team had a few automatic weapons, grenade launchers, and some RPGs.

The federal column was miles long with the tanks in the lead followed by the trucks carrying the infantry and their equipment and supplies. Dispersed among the trucks were Stryker vehicles to protect the trucks. The first team deployed by Blake had RPGs and fired on the lead tanks, knocking out the treads on two of them. That caused the column to come to a halt while infantry was bought up and dismounted from their transport vehicles to search the woods along the highway for the attackers. However, the small militia force was long gone, moving south through the woods to a position on the other side of the next two teams.

The second team was stationed about three miles down the highway and would not attack the tanks. The initial hit had caught the feds by surprise, and because the tanks had their turrets and guns pointed forward, they were not able to immediately return fire on the attackers in the woods. Blake knew that this would not be the case for the next assault. The tank turrets would be alternating and be pointed toward both sides of the road so they could launch devastating fire at the positions of any incoming fire from the militia.

For that reason, the second team of Blake's men let the tanks roll by their position along the highway and then opened fire with grenade launchers and automatic weapons on the more vulnerable trucks packed with enemy troops and, in some cases, supplies and ammunition. This particular team was led by a blond young, twenty-eight-year-old man named Robert Williams who was a first sergeant in the militia and second in command of Blake's special operations team, but his story was different from most of the other leaders of the militia special operations units.

Bobby Williams had no prior military experience. His family owned a cattle ranch outside of Canton, and when Bobby had graduated from high school, he had been preparing to go to Texas A&M University on a football scholarship. He also was planning to join the air force ROTC and hopefully become a pilot. Unfortunately, his dream ended the summer before his freshman year when his father was kicked in the head by one of the horses on the ranch. The injury was severe and caused the elder Robert Williams to lose the use of his legs. Since the younger Bobby was the only son in the family, he felt obligated to take over the operation of the ranch in order to take care of his parents and two younger sisters.

Bobby was highly intelligent and hardworking. Within a few years, he had made the ranch even more profitable than before, and he was able to hire some help. After the EMP attack, he was therefore able to join the East Texas militia and volunteer for special operations training. He was an excellent marksman and a fast learner, so he did exceeding well during the rigorous training. He had also proven himself to be a very valuable member of the team he was assigned to as they conducted both recon patrols and combat patrols to destroy enemy troops and capture their vehicles and equipment.

He was quickly elevated to the rank of first sergeant and second in command of Blake's team. Now he was commanding his own team made of other special operations and Louisiana militia members. He had deployed his men carefully. He had two grenade launchers, and the men who would fire them were on each side of him at the northern edge of the line. His riflemen were deployed to his south, and they would not open fire until the grenades hit their targets. After the tanks had passed his position, he allowed several Strykers to go by that were behind the tanks, but in front of the following trucks and Humvees. Bobby had seen that the Strykers both had 50-caliber machine guns, so he was not going to take them on.

Instead, he waited until they were far enough along that they could not return immediate fire on his team. He then ordered his men to open up on the trucks. The two men with the grenade launchers hit the first and second trucks that were passing in front of their position and both exploded in a ball of fire. Bobby used his M16 to first kill the driver of the third truck and then started firing into the canvas cover on the rear of the truck where either infantry or supplies were located. In this case, it was infantry, and those that were not hit by the initial rounds were jumping from the back of the truck. The same was happening with the other trucks taking fire from the remaining members of Bobby's team.

The sergeant had given clear instructions to his men to fire empty their rifle clips at the dismounted infantry and then quickly disengage before the enemy could get organized and effectively return fire and start moving into the woods. The attacks were taking place at night, so once again, the muzzle flashes of the militia weapons would give away their locations. Before this could be used against them, the team was to retreat into the deep woods and gather at a predetermined rendezvous point. They would then leapfrog past the other two teams to set up another ambush.

The men were obeying, and the withdrawal was being made in an orderly fashion, but Bobby saw something that caused him to linger for a few extra moments. The burning trucks had the area brightly illuminated, and Bobby noticed that there was very little return fire coming from the infantry who had left the trucks. Most of them had instead run into the woods on the other side of the road in order to hide. He could see some regular federal officers trying to rally the men and get them organized but generally were being ignored. Clearly, there was confusion among the enemy, and it could not all be explained by the success of the militia attack.

Bobby suspected that something else was going on, and he immediately recognized two possibilities. He knew that most of these soldiers were from Middle Eastern countries, but they were commanded by federal officers who were Americans working for the new government. Either the foreign soldiers were ill trained, or because most spoke no English they did not understand the orders being yelled at them by the federal officers, or they were getting the translations of the orders from their own officers and ignoring them. Either way, Bobby was immediately aware that the force headed for Texas was not as formidable as was first thought, at least as far as the quality of the combat troops was concerned.

CHAPTER XXIII

Captain Blake's teams conducted two more quick ambushes before regrouping and moving to the river so they could be ferried across before the sun came up. The combined attacks had accomplished exactly what was needed: the destruction of several tanks and Strykers as well as some supplies and the killing or wounding of scores of enemy troops. Just as important was the slowing down of the federal advance. To prevent further devastating attacks, the federal commander was forced to deploy a large portion of his infantry to lead the column. They were on the road itself and along both sides of the road. This meant that the column could move no faster than the infantry could walk.

This brought the militias in both Louisiana and Texas valuable time. The butcher's bill had been three members of the Louisiana militia killed and seven men wounded, including one of the East Texas special operations team members. No one was left behind. Blake's team brought back both their dead and the wounded. Now it was time for the second part of the plan to be put in motion.

No more attacks were launched on the federal column, and it was allowed to cross the Sunshine Bridge unimpeded. The federal troops quickly occupied the city of Donalsonville, and the English-speaking members of the federal force started questioning the residents about the whereabouts of the Louisiana National Guard units they were looking for. The population was uncooperative, and everyone claimed ignorance of any guard units in the area and also claimed that there was not a militia in the area either.

The federal commander, Colonel Jacob Collins, was a heavyset balding fifty-eight-year-old former federal bureaucrat, who was a devote progressive and had serious political ambitions, so he quickly became frustrated and was preparing to order his troops to resort to torturing residents and threatening their families in order to get the information he needed. It turned out not to be necessary because a teenage boy walked up early the next morning and handed an envelope to one of the federal officers near the commander's headquarters. The young man quickly disappeared, but when the envelope was opened, it contained exactly what the feds were looking for. In it was a handwritten letter from someone claiming to be a federal loyalist who could not reveal his identity for fear of reprisals by the other residents of the town.

The anonymous letter writer said that he knew the location of four National Guard units that were hiding out on a remote island in the Atchafalaya Swamp. The envelope also contained a crude map of the route to the hideout. However, the letter did not provide any specific information about the type of units that were at the location or their strength. Colonel Collins was not going to accept this letter on its face and immediately ordered a recon patrol of eighteen men in three armored Humvees to follow the route contained on the map. The patrol returned within twenty-four hours and told the colonel that it followed the road to within two hundred yards of the first bridge on the map and then deployed the infantry to check it out. They found nothing at the first bridge, so the column had proceeded to the second bridge about five miles down the road. When the infantry carefully approached that bridge, they found a heavily armed and manned roadblock consisting of over twenty men in Louisiana National Guard uniforms with a machine gun position set up covering the approach to the bridge.

This information appeared to confirm what the letter had stated, and now the colonel had to decide on a course of action. His major problem was that he knew virtually nothing about the strength of the units he would be attacking. He also did not know if they were just infantry units or if they had armor or even helicopters. He had no air support available at this point in his advance. There were some attack helicopters and fighter jets stationed at the New Orleans International Airport, but they were to support his attack on the East Texas militia—nothing else.

Aircraft fuel was a precious commodity in North America, as was gasoline. Prior to the EMP attacks, the federal government had been focused on the politics of climate change even though that theory had been discredited. That had resulted in most of the oil production and refining operations in the United States being either severely curtailed or completely shut down. The outcome had been that the United States relied almost entirely on imports of foreign gasoline and aviation fuel. With wars raging all over Europe and the Middle East, many countries were reluctant to part with fuel unless they were paid extremely well. Since the US economy was chaotic at best, there was only a limited supply of fuel of any type, especially aviation fuel. Therefore, air operations were limited for the federal units.

Colonel Collins decided that since he did not know what he was facing at the hunting camp and could be in for a major battle, he would commit a large portion of his force to the attack. The rest would be left in the Donaldsonville area to protect his rear against any possible militia activity and to act as a reserve force if needed. He had already lost two tanks and three Strykers to the militia ambush, so he decided to send in twenty of his remaining tanks, ten mobile artillery vehicles, and ten Strykers along with two battalions of infantry, over nine hundred men, to overwhelm the National Guard units. He felt that such a force would have no problem regardless of the strength of the guard.

CHAPTER XXIV

The next morning, just after dawn, the advance guard of the federal force approached the bridge across the first of the bayous on the road leading to the hunting camp. As had been reported by the recon patrol the day before, the bridge was unguarded, but the colonel had his men check under the bridge to make sure it was not rigged with explosives. They found nothing, so the column proceeded down the road.

There were five tanks in the lead followed by three Strykers and three trucks transporting infantry. The plan was to have the tanks destroy the roadblock at the second bridge and kill all the militia guards. The whole column would then proceed rapidly to the island where the tanks would open fire on the guard units while the infantry deployed to support them. They would be followed by five more tanks, more Strykers and Humvees with infantry, and five vehicles containing the 105mm artillery pieces. This initial assault force would be laying down significant firepower and would be quickly followed by the rest of the force.

When the leading elements approached the National Guard roadblock at the second bridge, it quickly became clear that it had been abandoned. The assault force commander, a federal captain, assumed that his column had been spotted early on, and the squad guarding the bridge had retreated to the island to alert the guard units. He radioed Colonel Collins who was in a Humvee following the assault units and told him of his suspicions.

The colonel had to make a snap decision. Withdrawal was not an option, so the column could either slow down and cautiously approach the island or move swiftly to try to engage the enemy before they could deploy into a strong defensive position. He chose the latter course of action and ordered the captain to speed up and quickly move to the attack. It never occurred to anyone to check this second bridge for explosives, but ultimately, it would have made no difference.

The tanks and other vehicles in the assault force covered the three remaining miles to the island in just a few minutes and started to deploy according to the original plan. The captain could see the hunting camp on the island just a few hundred yards away. It consisted of a large building that contained sleeping quarters for almost fifty hunters, a kitchen, and dining and lounge area. There were several outbuildings that included dog pens and two apparent storage sheds.

There was no sign of life, and none of the buildings appeared to have been used for quite a while. In addition, there was no sign of any fortifications, and the federal units were not taking any fire. The young captain felt like he had been kicked in the gut because he instantly knew that they had been duped. However, before he could even radio Colonel Collins and warn him, the captain heard two massive explosions to his rear. Both bridges had been simultaneously blown up and completely destroyed.

The explosive charges planted on both bridges had been placed on the parts of the structural beams that were below the water in the bayous. Therefore, the federal forces could not have found them with a search like they had done at the first bridge. The day before, while members of the militia had been manning the phony roadblock on the second bridge, members of Roger Hall's special operations team had used scuba gear to plant C-4 explosives on the bridges. They were set off remotely by team members hidden in the nearby swamps after the federal column had taken the bait and been lured into the ambush.

Colonel Collins now had a hell of a mess on his hands. He had been between the two bridges when the explosions had occurred, and by the time he had inspected both sites, he found that not only had the bridges been destroyed, but additional IEDs had been set off on either side of both bridges. He had lost two more tanks, two Strykers, and several dozen infantry. Three-fourths of his column was now trapped because both bridges crossed deep bayous. They could not be crossed by vehicles although soldiers could easily swim across them unless they were carrying equipment. There was no other way out.

The original federal force was now divided into three parts. There was the large contingent that was trapped by the fallen bridges, a much smaller contingent made up a few Strykers and about two hundred infantry and their vehicles that had not crossed either bridge, and then the part of the federal force that had been left in Donaldsonville. None of these components had any bridge-building equipment, and although a request had soon been made to the New Orleans headquarters, it had not been immediately replied to.

It was almost a week later that a courier arrived from New Orleans and informed the federal garrison commander in Donalsonville that it would be at least another week before contractors would arrive on-site with sufficient equipment to build two pontoon bridges across the bayous. This was good news for Collins, but it did not solve his immediate problem. His trapped men had quickly run out of food and fresh water, and they were now relying on supplies being ferried across the first bayou in small boats. To make matters worse, an unusually early winter storm had moved into the area and the men were now cold and wet.

On Ray's plantation outside of Donaldsonville, Daniel and his tactical militia commander Frank Hebert met with the two East Texas militia commanders, Norman Blake and Roger Hall, to discuss what their next move would be. Their primary mission had been accomplished. They had delayed the movement of the federal force toward Texas for at least several weeks. There was still an opening for further damage to be done. They could have ambushes set up to limit the supplies being brought to the trapped federal forces, and they could try to ambush any relief column coming up from New Orleans.

There were several problems with this approach. First, the feds would be expecting this and be better prepared to meet any such attacks than they had been for the ambush in the swamp. This made it questionable if the attacks would do much good, and they could be costly to the militia forces. The second problem of more concern was that there was still a sizable federal force occupying Donaldsonville, and so far, there had been no reprisals against the civilian populations. That was primarily because Daniel knew of several federal supporters in the city who would probably tell the feds anything they knew. So one of them was allowed to overhear a casual conversation in a bar about a rumor that there was a large force of East Texas militia in the Donaldsonville area. The ruse was to keep the feds from believing that the attack on their forces was the work of local militia.

That appeared to be working so far, but if the attacks were continued and any members of the militia were captured, it could all fall apart. With this in mind, the leaders agreed that there would be no more attacks on the feds. The Texas units would return to Canton, and the militia would melt back into the local population.

CHAPTER XXV

When the team leaders reported back to General Donnelly, he was elated at the outcome. He had some serious time now before his troops had to engage an invasion force from the east. The Donaldsonville militia would notify the Texas militia when the feds were on the move again. Since he had that time, Donnelly decided to do what he was known for, be proactive, and go on the attack. The target would be the federal force on the western border of the militia-controlled area.

He would draw up a plan of action and present it to his senior staff the next day. However, he had another meeting first. Ray Thibodeaux and the general's son Jamie had sent word that they had something important to give to the renowned commander. When they showed up at the general's office, Donnelly immediately hugged his son and congratulated him on passing the physical tests so he could start his training to be a special operations soldier in the militia. He told Jamie how proud he was of him, and Jamie now knew that he had truly been accepted back into the family.

Then the general sat down with him and Ray. Donnelly had seen that Ray was carrying something triangle shaped wrapped in plain brown paper, and he was curious to know what this was all about. Ray laid the package on the general's desk and told him that it had been found by Jamie and retrieved by him despite the danger involved for him personally. Ray then took off the cover, and Ben Donnelly saw the 9/11 flag. The general could not contain himself. He reached out and picked up the flag and gazed at it while tears welled up in his eyes.

With the exception of the original Star-Spangled banner, there was no other flag more precious to true Americans than the 9/11 flag. It had become even more important because the Star-Spangled banner that had flown over Fort McHenry in Baltimore, Maryland, in 1814, where a major battle had taken place during the war of 1812, and the flag had eventually been enshrined in the American History Museum of the Smithsonian Institution. Unfortunately, that flag had been removed from the museum and disappeared. The progressive federal government had deemed it to be "politically incorrect" because it had been flown during a time when slavery was still legal in the United States.

It was all part of the politically correct movement to demonize America, its institutions, and traditions so that the children in the United States could be raised to believe they lived in an evil country that was responsible for most of the ills in the world. That effort required a rewriting of American history to provide an interpretation of the Constitution and even the Declaration of Independence that declared them to be documents of oppression instead of those of freedom. The PC movement declared that the protection of things like freedom of speech, freedom of religion, freedom of the press, and especially the right to keep and bear arms were weapons of racism and tyranny and therefore must be abolished, along with all the symbols of the government that was supposed to protect those freedoms.

The American flag had ultimately been banned entirely, and its display was a criminal offense punishable by death. Ironically, the new federal government was not able to come up with a permanent flag to represent the new nation it was claiming to have become. The progressives from the gay community wanted their rainbow flag to be the new national flag; however, that was abhorrent to the radical Muslim community that wanted the black flag of ISIS to be the new national banner. Other racial and ethnic groups demanded that the new flag represent their interests and political agenda. Thus, the new order government had no flag, and this was just one of the indications that all was not well in the progressive paradise. Another such indication was the disorder and confusion among the federal forces that had been seen by Sergeant Bobby Williams during the attack on the enemy convoy.

On the other hand, Ben Donnelly knew that the flag he was holding in his hands was already a unifying force for the American people, and it would be treasured by the people of East Texas, particularly the militia. It gave them one more thing to fight for, and it would lead them into battle. The next day Donnelly had the flag raised in the Canton town square with members of the militia and local civilians present. It flew for twenty-four hours under guard and then was lowered and transported to each county seat of all the counties controlled by the militia. It was ceremoniously raised at each city and then taken to the next location. Then it was returned to Canton where it was to be kept flying over the beautiful, somber Van Zandt County Veterans Memorial until it truly became battle tested in the upcoming battle with the feds.

CHAPTER XXVI

As promised, the general had met with his staff and told them to draw up a plan of attack on the federal force on the border of Kaufman County and Dallas County. He wanted this force destroyed before the militia had to face the other threat from the east. However, after reviewing the reports of the recon patrols that had mapped out the encampment of the federal forces, Donnelly saw an opportunity available and decided to alter the plan. The federal commander on the border of Kaufman County, like his counterpart Colonel Jacob Collins, was obviously a political appointee who had no military background. He had certainly received some training before receiving his command, but it was not enough to keep him from making a basic mistake. He had set up a large tent city where his troops and gang members were housed and a separate motor pool several hundred yards away where all but a few of his vehicles were located. The recon patrol saw that there were many pickup trucks, some two-and-a-half-ton military trucks, over two dozen armored Humvees, and six heavily armed Strykers. The federal commander was smart enough to have the positions heavily guarded.

According to the intelligence gathered by the militia patrols, many of the trucks were covered and could contain additional weapons, ammunition, food, and fuel. If that was the case, then this could be a valuable acquisition for the militia; but even if there were no supplies, the vehicles would still be an important supplement to the militia inventory of vehicles and armor. Donnelly decided to send in an additional recon patrol made up of a special forces team to find out more.

The patrol was made up of another special operations team commanded by First Lieutenant Jack Dawson, a tall, muscular, and highly capable former marine recon platoon leader. His team had two jobs to do. The first was to try to infiltrate the enemy motor pool and find out what, if anything, were actually in the trucks and to determine where the guards were, what their pattern was, and when the guards were relieved and replaced. The second was to make sure that there had been no reinforcements of the Iranian reserve force.

When Dawson's team moved across the Kaufman County line early on a moonless Saturday night, they set up positions where they could monitor the guards of the motor pool. The first guard unit relief occurred at 8:00 p.m. and the next six hours later at 2:00 a.m. Once the relief had occurred, Jack let a few hours go by so the guards would not be alert as they were at first, and he sent in two of his team members who now knew the routine of the guards and were able to infiltrate the motor pool easily. What they found was stunning.

Some of the trucks were empty, so they were clearly used to carry troops, but others were full of food and fuel. Still, others contained weapons such as machine guns, RPGs, mortars, and ammunition. What the troops also saw was that the vehicles, including the Strykers and Humvees, all had their keys in their ignitions. The federal commander apparently had no real fear of an attack by the militia since he thought they would be occupied with protecting their eastern boundaries, and he wanted to be ready to move instantly when he received the attack order from his superiors. He obviously had not received the word that the federal advance in the east was stalled.

After the team confirmed that the strength of the Iranian reserve force had not changed, it returned to Canton and reported to the general. Donnelly was now ready to move. He met with his staff and told them how he wanted the operation to unfold. Within twenty-four hours, the details of the plan had been finalized; and on a crisp fall night, it went into effect. In the middle of the night, two battalions of the militia were quietly moved into the defensive positions maintained by the reinforced Kaufman County militia. However, their mission was offensive, not defensive. They would attack the federal forces but not before the militia air power had been deployed.

That would take place after the first phase of the operation was successfully completed. That initial phase consisted of the two special operations teams commanded by Jack Dawson and Norman Blake supported by two militia platoons taking control of the enemy motor pool. At 4:20 a.m., just an hour before dawn, the special forces teams moved in and quietly killed all the guards of the federal motor pool. They did this by getting behind them, using one hand to cover their mouths, and their other hand using knives to either cut their throats or drive the knives into their kidneys. Either way, there would be no outcry to alert other guards. It was all quick and efficient.

Once the guards had been terminated, the militia infantry platoons were brought in to secure the motor pool perimeter. They were accompanied by other members of the militia who were prepared to drive the Strykers, Humvees, and other vehicles. They were moved into position to wait for phase two of the operation that consisted of the attack on the main federal encampment. The attack was initiated at dawn by three militia Apache attack helicopters just as the federal troops and their gangster mercenaries were stumbling out of their tents.

The Apaches came in side by side, opened fire on the federal position with their 30mm chain guns, and tore up the camp and its occupants. The chain guns were devastating, and over a hundred feds were killed or wounded in the first pass. The first three Apaches were followed by two more that added to the casualties. The enemy was hit so hard and so fast that they were only able to get off a few shots from small arms at the helicopters, and none of the choppers were hit.

As the Apaches flew off, the militia infantry began their attack on the camp. They were led by six tanks and eight Strykers all firing their machine guns at the dazed-and-confused enemy. Faced with this type of firepower and the advancing infantry battalions, the federal force disintegrated. Many of the gang members and federal troops ran toward the motor pool to try to get in the vehicles and escape. However, Blake and Dawson had their men in position.

As soon as the Apaches had launched their attack, some of the militia drivers had started moving the trucks out of the motor pool and into the safety of Kaufman County. Simultaneously, other drivers had mounted the enemy Strykers and armed Humvees and moved them into positions to provide fire support for the militia infantry and special operations teams. So as the enemy rushed toward the motor pool to get their vehicles, they were met with heavy automatic weapons fire that stopped them in their tracks.

The federal commander tried to have his men return fire to try to break through to the vehicles, but the gang members had seen enough. This type of fighting was not what they had been told to expect. They were used to attacking towns with poorly armed militias or mostly unarmed civilians. The gang leaders and their followers turned and ran toward nearby wooded areas or tried going west on Highway 80. The federal commander only had about a hundred men with him attacking the motor pool. The rest of his men had been attempting to defend the camp, but they had been quickly overrun and the remnants were also in full retreat. The help the feds had expected to arrive from the Iranian reserve unit to the west had not appeared.

CHAPTER XXVII

The Iranian reserve force was not coming to the aid of the main federal force because it had plenty of problems of its own. At approximately ten the night before, three militia Blackhawk helicopters had transported two more special operation teams, two infantry platoons, and a team of combat engineers with the equipment and explosives needed to set IEDs up along the highway. They were put down in a pasture near the highway but about three miles from the Iranian position. It had taken several trips by the Blackhawks to get everyone into the landing zone, but it was done quickly and efficiently, and the men moved into position.

The two special operations teams were deployed in sniper positions around the Iranian camp, and the infantry platoons set up ambushes along Highway 80. The engineers were busy setting up IEDs along the three-mile route between the Iranian camp and the militia positions. The two infantry platoons had the toughest job. They needed to face both east and west so they could stop the Iranian advance from the west and also kill the retreating federal troops and gang members trying to escape the attack on the main camp to the east.

The platoons were under the leadership of their company commander of B Company of the First Infantry Battalion, Captain Jonathan Martin. He was thirty-five years old, a US Army veteran, and a resident of Wills Point, Texas. He had been in business as an electrical contractor until the EMP attack had occurred. Since the power grid was shut down, Jonathan could no longer generate income from his primary job, but he had a ten-acre family farm that would at least provide his family with food.

Jonathan was a patriot and believed in the oath he had taken as a member of the US military "to protect and defend the

Constitution of the United States against all enemies, foreign and domestic." That oath had no expiration date, and Jonathan signed up to be a part of the East Texas militia and offered his services to convert many of the militia vehicles to use electric power instead of gasoline. He had seen the handwriting on the wall and had placed solar panels on his own home, which ended up supplying not only his own family but also militia vehicles with energy. This was being done in conjunction with other experts who had been able to convert additional vehicles to rely on natural gas, which was readily available in East Texas by the use of solar energy to pump the gas out of the ground. As a result, the militia was able to have a virtually unlimited supply of fuel for its ground vehicles.

Jonathan's contributions to this breakthrough had been critical to the militia, but Johnathan felt he had more to offer. He wanted to serve as a combat officer, and because of his record, he was granted the command of a militia company. Now he found himself in a position where he had only two of his platoons in a situation where they would have to fight on two fronts. He knew they were in for a hell of a fight.

The attack on the Iranian reserve position started at the exact moment that the Apaches initiated the assault of the federal positions along the Kaufman County line. This additional air assault came from the four Blackhawk helicopters. They did not have the firepower of the Apaches, but three of them had two heavy machine guns while the fourth one had two powerful Gatling guns. The Blackhawks did not have the capability of taking out the enemy tanks, but their assault did destroy many other Iranian vehicles and killed or wounded scores of troops.

As his position was under attack by the helicopters, the Iranian commander received a distress call from the federal commander on the border of Kaufman County. He knew that his primary responsibility was to reinforce and protect the federal unit. He ordered his tank commanders and crews to man their tanks and prepare to move out and ordered his infantry commanders to mount the remaining transport vehicles and follow the tanks. As the men who were to man the tanks ran toward their armor, they were cut down by the two special operations teams that had taken up sniper positions. They were spread out in the nearby tree line with some of them behind trees and others up in the trees. They all had weapons with infrared sniper scopes made by the Buchanan family.

Their first job was to keep anyone from reaching the tanks, and they were successful in killing most of the men headed for the armored vehicles. Only two feds made it, and only because they had been sleeping in a small tent just about twenty yards from their tank. The other two members of the crew had not survived. However, since all members of tank crews were cross-trained, two men could operate the tank. That meant that only one of the Iranian tanks could move out with the rest of the reserve force.

Once they had done what they could to disrupt the movement of the armor, the snipers turned their fire on anyone who seemed to be in positions of command either as officers or noncommissioned officers. They shot and either killed or wounded a number of them before the heavy return fire forced the teams to withdraw. They moved east to join up with Captain Jonathan Martin and his infantry. At this point, the Iranian commander ordered his men forward. He did not know what he was facing but felt that he needed to join his remaining troops up with the federal force on the Kaufman County border. He never made it because while he had not seen any further sign of the Blackhawks that had initially hit his camp, he was not prepared for the Apaches that had been hovering nearby, waiting on orders.

The Apache Squadron commander was told that only one tank was moving forward with the Iranian force, and it needed to be destroyed along with the vehicles carrying the Iranian infantry. However, only three Apache helicopters would be used because of the limited fuel and ammunition available. The choppers made one pass and fired several rockets in addition to using their chain guns. They took out the Iranian tank in the lead and three Strykers that were following in the column. They also killed and wounded many more Iranian soldiers who were riding in the trucks that survived the initial assault.

The remnants of the Iranian force continued down Highway 80 with only twelve vehicles and less than 150 men. They made it about two hundred yards before they ran into the first of the IEDs placed along the highway by the militia team of combat engineers. One of these destroyed the armored Humvee that the Iranian commander was riding in, and he died instantly. Since most of the other officers in the force had already been killed, the Iranian troops decided to turn around and go back up the highway to someplace safe. However, for most of them, there was no safety.

The militia special operations teams had been moving through the woods on the side of the road to hook up with Captain Martin and his men while at the same time shadowing the enemy column. When Roger Hall, who was commanding the teams, saw the Iranians turning back, he unleashed the full firepower of his teams on the retreating enemy. This was a no quarter fight. The American forces were facing several brutal enemies including the Iranian forces, the federal troops who were treasonous Americans betraying their own country, and the gang members who were rapists and murderers. Nome of them deserved mercy; and the militia was not going to take food, water, and medical supplies away from the American people to take care of prisoners, so no surrenders were accepted. The enemy troops were simply killed.

The same was true for the enemy that Captain Martin and his two infantry platoons were facing. A runner sent by Roger Hall had informed Martin that the Iranian threat no longer existed, so he was able to turn his attention entirely to the retreating federal force that had been driven away from the Kaufman County border. Martin had three squads deployed to defend the highway, and the rest of the men were stretched out in a defensive line in the woods on both sides of the road. Martin knew that some of the enemy would be trying to escape through the woods, and once the group on the road ran into his roadblock, many of them would also take to the woods.

In fact, the attack on the main federal camp had been very successful because many of the enemy had been killed, and the rest kept from reaching the vehicles in the motor pool. However, there had been several dozen trucks in the encampment itself, and some that survived militia attack were now being used to transport the federal soldiers and some of the gang members who were well aware that they were running for their lives. The retreat quickly turned disastrous because the militia engineers had also set up IEDs to the east of Martin's position.

These powerful explosive devices destroyed the first eight of the enemy vehicles approaching on the road and killed most of the occupants. This led to the rest of the vehicles being abandoned, and the enemy troops were determined to fight their way on foot through the militia lines. This put Martin and his men in a difficult position because he had less than ninety men facing almost three hundred of the enemy. Martin was the commander of an elite group of militia infantry, and he did what an officer in that position is required to do: lead his men. The militia was taking heavy fire all along the line, and so Martin moved among them, directing fire and encouraging his men to hold the line. His defense was bolstered when Roger Hall moved his commandos into the fight, but his force was still heavily outnumbered.

Captain Jonathan Martin did what he was trained to do and what he had taken an oath to do: lead his men to fight for their country and their Constitution. He continued to move along their defensive line, directing fire and encouraging his men to give an all-out effort. He saw some of them fall as the enemy onslaught continued, and then suddenly, this courageous commander fell to the ground. He had taken a bullet to the head that had killed him instantly.

A few minutes later, the captain's command was relieved when militia tanks supported by hundreds of militia infantry roared up Highway 80 and slammed into the rear of the retreating federal forces and their gang mercenaries. The militia cut them down. Captain Martin was not alive to see this or to see the lone Humvee that led the militia column. It was flying an American flag, the same flag that had been considered nothing more than a rag when first discovered by Jamie Donnelly. It was the 9/11 flag, and as General Ben Donnelly had promised, it had led the American attack.

CHAPTER XXVIII

Ray Thibodeaux had been offered the rank of lieutenant colonel in the militia and a job on the general's staff, but he had another assignment he requested first. He told General Donnelly that since the 9/11 flag was to lead the troops into battle, it would need to be heavily guarded by an elite team that would keep it from falling into enemy hands at all cost. Ray had volunteered to lead that team and asked that he be able to choose the team members. His commanding officer readily agreed, and then Ray requested that the general's son, Jamie, be a part of the team. He told Ben, "While I know Jamie has not yet completed his special operations training, I believe that since he is the man who found and saved this flag, he should be part of the team. He can resume his training after the battle." Once again, the general agreed.

Ray didn't have to go far to recruit the rest of his team; all the men who had escaped from New Orleans with him readily volunteered with the exception of Tim Johnson who was still recovering from the wounds he had received at the battle for the Sabine River Bridge. They flew the flag on a Humvee with six men inside to protect it and were followed by the Stryker with the rest of the team. It was positioned right behind the American lines on the Kaufman County border until it was time for the infantry and armor to move forward to the attack. Then the vehicles drove into a position where they were following the armor but in full view of and leading the militia infantry.

The Humvee carrying the flag had received some sporadic fire, but the enemy had been too preoccupied with trying to get away from the devastating American attack to worry about an American flag on a Humvee. They might have felt differently if they had known that the very sight of this flag had caused the hearts of the patriot soldiers to swell with pride and fight with all their strength to achieve victory.

It had been a great and decisive victory for the East Texas militia. Of the original combined forces of federal and Iranian troops and their gang mercenaries, less than two hundred had escaped. The rest were dead with the exception of a few officers who were captured so they could be interrogated. There were also three gang members released but only after they witnessed their fellow murderers and rapists lined up and shot. The three were allowed to live so they could take a clear message back to their fellow gang members in Dallas. Joining up with the federal forces was not a good idea.

General Donnelly was congratulated by his staff for his audacious and highly successful plan. Not only had it destroyed many enemy soldiers, but the militia now had three more heavy tanks and several dozen Strykers and Humvees; numerous automatic weapons; thousands of rounds of ammunition, grenades, and RPGs; and truckloads of fuel, food, and medical supplies.

General Donnelly accepted the congratulations, but it was a bittersweet victory for him. Sixty-two members of the militia had died in the battle, and 118 more had been wounded. Among the dead was Captain Jonathan Martin who had been personally appointed to command what became to be one of the best infantry companies in the militia and who left behind a wife and two young children. It had always been the practice in the past that when members of the militia were killed, General Donnelly would personally visit their families and attend the funerals of his fallen soldiers. He would also visit the wounded being cared for in the medical facilities. However, his troops had never suffered casualties of this magnitude, and since he now had to turn his attention in the federal threat in the east, he would not be able to do what he considered to be his duty to the fallen.

With the western border secured, General Donnelly returned to his headquarters in Canton to find out what his recon units had learned about the enemy advance coming up through Louisiana. He learned that the federal forces had successfully completed the pontoon bridges over the bayous and the entire federal force was together again. However, the force commander Colonel Jacob Collins had been blamed for the debacle, had been relieved of his command, and had been executed. Failure was not an option tolerated by the federal government.

The new federal commander of the column went by the name of Raphael Ortega but was, in fact, actually Omar Shala, a plant by the Muslim Brotherhood who had worked undercover inside the federal government for years. In order to undermine and ultimately destroy the Constitutional Republic that was the United States, the progressives were willing to make allies of anyone that could assist in that endeavor, including the Muslim Brotherhood that had its own agenda to force Sharia law on the entire world.

Shala had originally been given a high-level position in the Department of Homeland Security where he was supposed to be specializing in tracking foreign terrorists trying to infiltrate the United States. Instead, he was given the task of having all US military veterans as declared potential domestic terrorists and placed on the terror watch list and, in many cases, on the no-fly list and then having their firearms seized. Since the concept of "due process" required by the Constitution had been essentially done away with, Shala was highly successful, and millions of America's heroes were stripped of their constitutional rights.

Shala was rewarded for his success by being appointed a colonel in the federal army, but his cover was maintained because even some progressives were getting uneasy over the increasing use of troops from Muslim countries to subdue American citizens. These progressives wanted to be in control, not relinquish it to those who would declare Sharia law so they could be in control.

So Omar Shala continued to be Colonel Raphael Ortega, who was placed in command of the Syrian soldiers in the Louisiana column, because he had supposedly been trained to speak Arabic—which was, in fact, his native language—and could better communicate with the troops. Shala was a small man, only five feet eight inches tall, and with a swarthy complexion that could belong to a man of Middle Eastern descent or someone from Mexico or

Central America. He was good at everything he did, but he was also a committed jihadist and was sadistic and brutal. He was about to prove that.

The successful militia attack on the federal force on the western border of the East Texas militia was devastating to the plan to invade the militia-held territory form the east. The Louisiana federal column was still strong despite the loss of a large number of tanks and other vehicles as well as several hundred troops. However, there was a major problem: they did not know what they might be facing if they invaded East Texas. The feds now knew that the East Texas militia had armor and helicopter support, but they had no real idea of the true militia strength.

Thus, the federal command decided to withdraw its force back to New Orleans until it could be reinforced. Shala was not content with just withdrawing his force. He did not believe that the attacks on the federal force were just the result of actions by the East Texas militia. He knew that they must have had help from people in and around the Donaldson area, but he didn't have the time or resources to find out who was involved, and it didn't matter to him anyway. Guilty or innocent, they were all infidels, and that is what he said to two platoons of his Syrian troops when he sent them into the town in the middle of the night.

They kicked in doors; shot men, women, and children in their own homes; and then set the houses on fire. The raid was not as successful as Shala had hoped, however. He had wanted to commit his tanks and more men, but fuel and ammunition were precious and must be preserved for the upcoming fight against the Texas militia. So his raiding force was relatively small, and it was not unexpected. Local police, sheriff's deputies, and militia had been on patrol and responded as soon as the first shots were reported. The Syrian troops had been ordered to conduct a brutal strike and then quickly withdraw to avoid a firefight with the locals. They did withdraw but not before losing over a dozen men to the outraged community.

Twenty-three residents of the Louisiana city had been killed and many others wounded, and the message that Colonel Shala had sent had been received, but the reaction was not what he wanted. He had unleashed terrorism on the city, but while it caused grief and shock, it also infuriated the population; and overnight, the relatively small militia had hundreds of new recruits. Daniel and Frank Hebert had adopted the training techniques of the East Texas militia and soon became so strong that no one from the federal government dared to enter the parish.

CHAPTER XXIX

The word of the victory over federal forces by the East Texas militia had spread quickly throughout the country; and it was encouraging other resistance forces to become better trained, stronger, and more aggressive. The feds were receiving more pressure than ever before in states all around the former United States of America, and it was determined that the only way to reverse the trend was to totally destroy the East Texas militia as soon as possible.

In Canton, Texas, General Ben Donnelly had been relieved to find out that the federal column that was threatening the eastern border of Texas had withdrawn to New Orleans to await reinforcements. This gave the general more time to build his strength and try to come up with a plan to meet what he knew would probably be the greatest threat yet.

The victory over the federal forces in Kaufman County had not only supplied the militia with much-needed equipment and supplies and had also brought in many new recruits. Temporary housing had been constructed for the new men and women, and because there were so many active farms and ranches in the area that were not being taxed by the federal government, there was an adequate supply of food for everyone. What was not readily available were the weapons and ammunition needed to equip these troops.

More combat patrols were sent out to attack federal positions and seize weapons and supplies; and the Buchanan family had many volunteers assisting them in their armory to make firearms, hand grenades, mortars, and mortar rounds. They were also manufacturing artillery rounds for the few artillery pieces that the militia had. Artillery was something they were desperately short of, and it was needed to mount an effective defense to a federal invasion. A Marine Corps reserve artillery unit based near Houston had managed to escape the feds and get to the militia-controlled counties with four 105mm howitzers and some ammunition. There were also veteran memorials and American Legion or VFW posts in the area that displayed artillery pieces, mostly 75mm artillery, but there were a few 105s. One of the 75mm guns was at the Van Zandt County Veterans Memorial.

The barrels of these artillery pieces had either been plugged or the firing mechanisms removed; but the Buchanan family, with the help of some local veterans, had been able to unplug them and recreate the missing firing mechanisms. However, while the 75mm and 105 pieces were good for use against infantry and lightly armored vehicles, they were not effective against heavy tanks. The militia needed heavier artillery but did not have the capability to manufacture it themselves.

However, General Donnelly knew where heavy artillery and more tanks were located not far from his militia border. They were at Fort Hood, Texas, that is just outside of the city of Killen in Bell County. That was only one county away from Limestone County that had recently come under the control of his militia. When the progressives that had taken control of the federal government were preparing to consolidate their power, they had to make sure that they were in control of military equipment and bases that could potentially be used against them. For years, they had been reducing the size of the military and getting rid of the members of the armed forces that they knew believed in the oath they had taken and would refuse to be involved in an effort to destroy the Constitution and refuse to obey any orders to fire on their fellow citizens to enforce the new order.

The federal government followed the same path that Adolf Hitler and other vicious dictators had followed. The path was to purge the military of anyone who was loyal to their country and its people and not to any individual or political party. The military personnel were purged, so they could be replaced by people loyal not to the United States but to the SRA leaders that were in control. These included illegal aliens, mercenaries, released criminals, and those who were true believers in the idea that there were certain people who were the elite and everyone else were their servants. Over the course of a little over a year, the men and women in the armor and artillery units at Fort Hood were separated from the army or shipped out to other bases and assigned to menial jobs.

They were replaced by federal troops that were to guard the base and its important equipment until it was needed to attack resistance units. Fort Hood was a very large base, over 158,000 acres; and because so many federal and hired foreign troops were being used to occupy rebellious states, there were only two federal companies assigned to guard the fort. One was a military police company, and the other was an infantry unit with some of its members trained as drivers so they could move the tanks and artillery when necessary. The base command was assigned to a federal major who once again had no prior military experience but was politically connected.

However, Major Jackson Sommers was not stupid. He knew he had less than five hundred men to guard the large military post, so he had all the tanks and artillery moved into the center of the base and the ammunition stored in a nearby armory. He and his superiors were concerned that militia might try to destroy or damage the tanks and artillery, but it never occurred to them that the militia was strong enough to try to steal the weapons. This assessment had not changed even when the East Texas militia destroyed the invasion force on its western border and captured most of the federal weapons and armor.

Major Sommers now had an additional concern that since the militia had used attack helicopters in the Kaufman County fight, they might use them to attack the tanks and artillery at Fort Hood. To protect against this possibility, Sommers requested and received the return of several antiaircraft batteries that had previously been part of the Fort Hood garrison. When General Donnelly heard of this new development, it did not deter him because his intention was not to use air power to wipe out the armor and artillery at Fort Hood but to use infantry to capture it. In fact, the possibility of capturing air defense artillery made the target more inviting than ever.

Fortunately, for the East Texas militia, there had not been extensive federal air strikes against the Canton area or other locations they controlled. The feds had soon learned that using their limited supply of aircraft fuel and munitions for such attacks was counterproductive. They could launch airstrikes against the civilian populations in the militia-controlled counties, but they were not able to do any significant damage to the military capabilities that were widely dispersed and hidden. As a result, the attacks were halted, but General Donnelly knew they would resume in order to support any major assault launched against the militia.

Antiaircraft units would be critical when that happened, but capturing them and the tanks and artillery in Fort Hood would not be easy. Donnelly knew that he would need to send in at least two full battalions to ensure the success of the assault. One battalion could succeed but would probably suffer heavy casualties while two battalions would be much more effective and reduce militia losses. He did not want to risk his helicopters unless absolutely necessary, and he didn't want to destroy the heavy equipment on the base. Therefore, this would have to be primarily an infantry operation supported by some Strykers and armored Humvees. Some tanks would also be available but again only be used in an emergency.

CHAPTER XXX

━━━◄◐◑►━━━

This operation had to be successful because of the risk involved, so it had to be carefully planned and quickly carried out since Donnelly did not know when the feds might be making another move against East Texas, and his militia had to be ready. It was also imperative that this operation be kept secret, so there would be no surprises when the assault on Fort Hood was made.

Donnelly put his entire command staff to work, planning the operation. They had complete plans of the base and recon teams had been able to pinpoint the location of the tanks, artillery, antiaircraft guns, and the infantry units guarding them. The staff now had to come up with a plan to get the militia units into attack positions without being spotted, launch a successful attack, and then get the units and hopefully the captured heavy equipment back to Canton safely.

The command staff had mostly been handpicked by Donnelly from the volunteers who had joined the militia at the very beginning of its formation. David McKay was the general's executive officer and in charge of supervising the rest of the staff. He had held the same position as a lieutenant colonel in the US Army's Second Ranger Battalion. In the army, the S-3 was the training and operations officer for commands all the way from the battalion level to the division level and beyond. During peacetime, the S-3 was responsible for training; but during wartime, the responsibility shifted to planning tactical operations. The militia needed both; so Donnelly had appointed Daniel Miller, a veteran Marine Corps gunnery sergeant, to supervise the training of the militia and Jacob McMillan, a retired US Army infantry major, to handle tactical operations.

The S-4 position was assigned to handle logistics for the militia. This included providing food, water, ammunition, weapons, and medical supplies for the entire militia. For that important assignment, Donnelly chose a retired navy commander Allison Mitchell, who had held that type of position aboard the aircraft carrier, *USS Ronald Reagan*, to handle the logistics for the rapidly expanding militia. The final position was that of S-2, the director of all military intelligence operations for the militia. That task was not initially assigned to a military veteran because the few who had intelligence experience did not appear to have the capability to be an S-4.

Instead, that job was given to Justin Smith, a former CIA agent with extensive experience in gathering intelligence through various methods. He was in charge of sending out recon patrols and assessing the intelligence they gathered so he could advise the general about any potential threats. He also assessed potential targets for offensive operations to be used to destroy enemy units and capture weapons and supplies. Smith's job was even more critical now that the militia was preparing a major operation against Fort Hood.

Smith reported that the recon patrols had found that after consolidating the weapons, heavy equipment, and personnel to the interior of the base, the west gate had been left totally unguarded, providing easy access to the base. There were a few guards posted farther down the street past the entrance, but they could easily be taken out by special operations personnel. It appeared to be the perfect place for the infantry to launch their attack on the base.

Based on this information, Donnelly ordered his staff to start planning the attack and give him a timeline. The senior staff assembled their teams and got to work early in the morning. Twelve hours later, they all met with the general and laid out the proposed plan. As the general had expected, two infantry battalions would be deployed against the base in a coordinated attack but only after two special operations teams had cleared the approach of any guards.

The attack would be led by four Strykers carrying a full infantry platoon and five armored Humvees with additional infantry squads. They would be the assault troops followed by dismounted infantry. One company of infantry would be held in reserve with four Bradley tanks. Also in reserve would be five Blackhawk helicopters and three Apache gunships in case the attack went badly and there were troops who needed to be extracted or supported by gunships.

Once the base had been captured, the extraction would begin of the troops and captured armor and artillery with the helicopters standing by to provide cover. Different evacuation routes would be used so that all the units would not be on the same highways or roads at the same time. This was the crux of the plan, but they spent several hours going over every detail, and considering every possible thing that could go wrong and every possible contingency plan to deal with such possibilities. Finally, the staff agreed on a plan and General Donnelly approved it.

It would take several days for the men and equipment to be gathered, provisioned, and supplied; and then because the movement to the Fort Hood area had to be cautious and meticulous, it would take at least five days to move all the units into position. The first part of the plan went fine with all units equipped within forty-eight hours and they were ready to move. Then, the general unexpectedly called an emergency staff meeting. The staff assembled at their headquarters in the old Canton courthouse located in the town square.

The meeting was a surprise to the staff members and their teams, but they believed that the general just had some final instructions. However, what they actually heard came as a complete shock to them. Their beloved commander announced that he had second thoughts about the attack on Fort Hood and was cancelling the operation. However, he proposed another operation that he believed was less risky. He told his staff that he had received information from a source in a county near Houston that the federal forces had established a munitions depot about one hundred miles south of Fort Hood. The general ordered his staff to draw up a new plan to attack and seize these munitions.

His staff complied, but some of them were concerned with this turn of events. It did not make sense, and they wondered if their commanding general had lost his edge and become overly cautious. In fact, General Donnelly knew that there would be concerns over his decision, but he had no choice. He had a source inside of Fort Hood that he had not shared with anyone else on his staff. His contact was Jordan Billings, a young man who had been an Eagle Scout in the Boy Scout troop that the general had been the scoutmaster of years earlier.

Eagle Scouts had been trained to be patriots, and Jordan had been no exception. He had gone to college at the University of Texas, obtained a degree in criminal justice, and upon graduation had joined the Department of Homeland Security. He had quickly advanced because of his dedication and hard work. Yet he had also become concerned that the agency he served seemed to be becoming less interested in protecting his country and more interested in destroying the Constitutional Republic that he had sworn an oath to protect.

He was preparing to resign from the agency when he heard about the building resistance to the new federal order. At that point, it occurred to him that he might be more effective as an inside source to support the resistance. He stayed with the agency as its members were converted into the federal police force and then a full-blown military operation to subdue the American people after the EMP attack. Eventually, Jordan found himself as a captain in the federal force guarding Fort Hood. He was, in fact, second in command of the two companies in the fort and was completely trusted by Major Sommers.

However, the major was not aware that Jordan had made contact with the local militia commander in Waco, Texas. It had happened by accident, when Jordan had been at a local bar in Killeen, Texas, that was the town right outside of the post. He had entered the bar in civilian clothes while off duty because he knew that anyone wearing the uniform of the federal troops would be viewed with suspicion. He knew that he was possibly putting himself in a dangerous situation, but he was desperate to try to make contact with the militia since he had just learned in a briefing on the base that his former scoutmaster was the commander of the East Texas militia.

As Jordan sat at the bar drinking a beer, he glanced around and saw a familiar face sitting at a table with three other men in a corner of the barroom. The man he saw was Corey Davidson, his former college roommate at the University of Texas. It didn't take long for Corey to glance in Jordan's direction and immediately recognize him. However, Corey also knew that his friend and roommate had gone to work for the Department of Homeland Security after graduation, so he became concerned for his own safety and that of the three men with him who were all members of the Killeen militia that was operating in a county that was still controlled by the feds.

Corey told his comrades to leave, and as they walked out of the door, the handsome young redhead approached Jordan with a big smile on his face. "How are you, old buddy?" he asked. "What are you doing here in this neck of the woods?"

"Just here on business," said Jordan as he ordered drinks for him and his friend and then suggested that they move to a table away from the bar. Jordan had made a quick decision that could cost him his life. He knew that Corey was a fellow Eagle Scout and as such a patriot, so he decided to confide in him. He told Corey why he was in the area and that he was still loyal to the United States and its Constitution and wanted to contact the local militia and eventually his former scoutmaster, General Donnelly. He told Corey, "I know you and I believe you are probably a militia member or at least know the leaders, so I'm asking for your help."

Jordan could tell that Corey was hesitant, and he did not blame him. He would probably feel the same way if their positions were reversed, so he decided to try something. In addition to being fellow Eagle Scouts, both men had also been Vigil members of the Boy Scout Order of the Arrow honor society. This was a group reserved for the best of the scouts; and there were three levels: Ordeal members, Brotherhood members, and Vigil members. Vigil membership was the highest level a scout could receive, and it was not given to many members.

The Order of the Arrow was a secret society with rituals going back to those of the Delaware Indian tribe. Each level had a secret handshake done with the left hand, and in the case of Vigil members, it was the ultimate expression of trust. Jordan offered his left hand to Corey, and they exchanged the secret handshake. The bond of trust was established, and Corey told his old friend that he would let General Donnelly know that Jordan would be providing information about what occurred at Fort Hood.

CHAPTER XXXI

Corey sent word to General Donnelly that he had a source inside the fort and wanted instructions on how to handle this asset. The general told Corey to come to Canton so they could talk in person. This was easily done since one of the advantages that the East Texas militia had over many of the federal units was the fact that there was almost an unlimited supply of natural gas in the counties controlled by the militia. Engineers had converted the militia vehicles to run on natural gas instead of standard gasoline that was still scarce, and Corey had one of these converted vehicles.

As a result, Corey Davidson was able to drive his pickup to Canton and meet personally with the general. When he found out that the source in Fort Hood was Jordan Billings, he was delighted. He remembered Jordan well and instinctively knew he could be trusted. He instructed Corey that it was important that he personally report all information from Jordan directly to him. It was not to go through the normal intelligence channels. This would be a private source for the general.

This was unusual for Donnelly because all intelligence was usually sent through his S-2, Justin Smith, and his intelligence staff. Unfortunately, the general had become concerned that there might be a traitor or mole in his staff. His concerns had started not long after the militia had successfully repulsed the potential invasion by federal forces coming through from Louisiana and Dallas County. Much of the intelligence that had supported that successful operation had come from the Donaldsonville militia with the assistance of the East Texas militia special operations and recon units working with them.

Since then, things had changed. Several East Texas militia recon patrols and one combat patrol had failed to report in or return from their assigned missions. It was not unheard of for patrols to run into problems. The vast majority of them were successful in their missions, and sometimes they would be involved in firefights that resulted in casualties, but the survivors of the patrols always returned. The general needed someone he could completely trust to find out if these losses had just been coincidences or deliberate actions by some member of the militia. He chose Ray Thibodeaux for the job.

Ray was now member of the general's staff assigned to assist in the training of personnel for the special operations teams. Donnelly quickly learned that he was highly intelligent and motivated. He also had two soldiers that had helped him and his team escape that were former Louisiana National Guard intelligence officers. Ray was asked to have his men monitor the members of the S-2's section to try to determine if there were leaks. Ray and his team started watching the movements of Justin Smith and the senior members of his intelligence staff.

The urgency of their investigation was increased by the fact that two recon patrols sent to the Fort Hood area had also failed to return. A week later, Ray Thibodeaux reported some disturbing information to the general: his S-2, Justin Smith, had a storage shed in Canton that had a radio antenna connected to it. His team had also found that Smith had been to the shed within hours after the recon patrols had been dispatched to the Fort Hood area.

While Donnelly was considering this revelation, Corey Davidson came to his headquarters to convey some critical information received from Jordan Billings. Jordan had conveyed to Corey that he had been part of a high-level briefing that stated that intelligence from a source inside the East Texas militia had provided details of a planned attack on Fort Hood. As a result of this information, the federal government had moved a full brigade of Iranian infantry, as well as two armored battalions to a position within a mile south of Fort Hood.

A carefully crafted trap had been laid for the destruction of the East Texas militia units when they attacked Fort Hood, but it would not be successful. All the communications by Justin

Smith were being monitored, and after General Donnelly made his startling announcement to his staff that the attack on Fort Hood was being aborted, Ray and his team were able to determine that this information had been sent to the federal command. They had followed Smith to the storage shed facility and monitored his radio broadcast that was in a simple code that the fully recovered Tim Johnson, and Jerry Calhoun had easily broken.

Once they confirmed that Smith had told his superiors about the change in plans announced by Donnelly, they did not arrest him but allowed him to continue to serve in his position on the general staff. Then were listening in several days later when he got on the radio again and informed the feds that, in fact, two battalions of militia and some supporting armor had moved out of Canton heading south toward a reserve center just north of Houston. Then, once again, they waited until Corey Davidson brought news to Donnelly from Jordan Billings that the feds had taken the bait. The Iranian infantry brigade and armored units had moved away from their positions near Fort Hood and were headed farther south toward the reserve center.

The staff was called to another meeting, and the general apologized for the ruse and explained the situation that had caused him to get them to change plans. He also informed them that Justin Smith was in custody. Not all the staff members had been kept in the dark, and the commander of the force that had been dispatched from Canton was also aware that there might be an immediate change in orders. When he received the new orders, the column made an abrupt turn to the west and headed back toward the original target at Fort Hood.

The whole situation had been stunning to the staff, and they could not believe that they had been betrayed by one of their own. Justin Smith was not talking yet, but his interrogations would continue, and they would not always be conducted in a politically correct manner. In the meantime, the staff returned to the most important matter at hand: the impending attack on Fort Hood. Because of the existence of the large Iranian force, extra precautions had to be taken. Even though the enemy force had moved to the south, it was only about a hundred miles away and could be back at Fort Hood within a few hours once it received word of the militia assault.

In order to prevent the Iranians from being able to reinforce the fort and/or interfere with the withdrawal of the captured equipment back to Canton, Donnelly dispatched a company of special operations units consisting of four A teams of twelve men each and a heavy weapons infantry platoon in support equipped with 81mm mortars, machine guns, and antitank weapons. It was a heavy commitment but necessary to support this critical mission.

For Donnelly, it was an even heavier personal commitment since his son Jamie had completed his training and was assigned to the A team commanded by Captain Robert Cannon. Jamie had been given a choice: he could accompany Ray Thibodeaux and his team as they guarded the 9/11 flag that would lead the attack on Fort Hood, or he could join an A team. It was a tough choice for Jamie because he was close to Ray and the men who had escaped from New Orleans together and to the flag that he had found and rescued. On the other hand, he felt obligated to fulfill the new job he was trained to do, and even more obligated to be in this fight with his brother Matt who was a combat engineer major assigned to support the special forces teams and set booby traps and IEDs to destroy or at least damage the Iranian armor.

In their younger days, Jamie had been very close to both of his brothers. They had all been Boy Scouts together and shared good times hunting and fishing with their father. That had ended when Jamie had decided to follow the path of the progressives who wanted to remake America. That separated him from the values of his family, and he was afraid they would never forgive him. However, not only has his father welcomed Jamie back into the family, but so had Matthew. They had become close again, but unfortunately, that had not yet happened with Jamie's brother John. This was not the fault of either of the brothers because when Jamie had reconnected with his father and brother Matthew, he found out that John, who was an Apache helicopter pilot, was off on some kind of special assignment for their father.

CHAPTER XXXII

The attack on Fort Hood started an hour before dawn on a cold December morning. Jordan Billings had received word from his friend Corey that his message about the Iranian withdrawal from the Fort Hood area had been received by General Donnelly. Corey had also informed Jordan when the attack would take place, and while it would be primarily on the poorly guarded west gate, there would be a diversionary attack on the east gate that was designed to draw the federal forces into positions to defend the east side of the fort.

Jordan was also told that if possible, he should do anything he could to get the diversion to work for as long as possible. Jordan knew exactly what he needed to do. When word came into the headquarters that there was an attack occurring at the east gate, Major Sommers ordered two platoons to reinforce the eastern perimeter while maintaining the rest of the force around the perimeter surrounding the armor, artillery, and antiaircraft units.

As the orders were executed so everyone in the command center left to lead their units except for Major Sommers, Lindsay Gordon, the command first sergeant, and Jordan who immediately pulled out his 9mm side arm and shot and killed both Sommers and his first sergeant. Now he was in command, and his orders to the rest of the federal force to move to the east gate were assumed to come from the commander. The killing of Sommers and the first sergeant had not been easy because they had both considered Jordan as friends, but both were rabid progressives who were totally committed to destroying the East Texas militia and end the resistance movement against the federal government. They were traitors to their own country, so Jordan did what he had to do.

He had ordered all the federal force to repel the attack at the east gate with the exception of one platoon to continue guarding the tanks and artillery. He suspected that leaving anything less than that might cause suspicion among the federal company commanders. By the time the majority of the federal troops had moved toward the east gate, which was over four miles from their current position, a special operations team attached to the main militia unit silently took out the federal guards near the western gate. The team once again used their knives, so no shots were fired, and the rest of the federal force did not get alerted to the attack through the west gate.

That allowed the Strykers and armored Humvees to quickly move down the street to the motor pool where the tanks and artillery were housed. They deployed around the perimeter and opened fire on the federal troops that were in prepared defensive positions consisting of redoubts made of sandbags. These could provide limited protection for the federal troops from machine gun and small arms fire but not from the grenade launchers that several of the Strykers were equipped with. They blew apart the redoubts, and that allowed the infantry that they were carrying to disembark and wipe out the remaining poorly trained federal troops that were no match for the highly trained militia.

All the tanks and artillery had quickly been captured, and several squads had been sent out to take over the antiaircraft batteries. This proved to be an easy task because while the crews had manned their guns, they were not prepared to defend them against infantry; and when they realized that they were being approached by militia, they abandoned their guns and took off running.

While this action was taking place, the rest of the federal troops thought they were in the process of routing the militia attack on the east gate. In reality, the militia troops were staging a controlled retreat, and the federal commanders realized that this might be the case when they heard heavy gunfire and explosions to their rear near the location of the critical equipment and vehicles they had been guarding. The senior federal commander decided to leave two platoons to hold the east gate and took his remaining men back to the west. They didn't get far before they ran into a full battalion of militia infantry that had moved forward after the capture of the federal armor and artillery.

The federal troops were also hit by the Strykers, armored Humvees, and special operations team that came in or their left flank. The feds tried to retreat in the face of the devastating attack but were blocked by the militia force moving in from the east gate. It had been reinforced by a reserve platoon and a Stryker. The feds were being cut to pieces, so they did something they knew was probably futile: they threw down their weapons and surrendered. The federal soldiers had all been made aware that the militia rarely took prisoners. However, much to their relief, their surrender was accepted, and they were soon being prepared to march back to Canton with the militia units that had captured them.

Events had recently occurred that had caused General Donnelly and his staff to rethink their approach to federal prisoners. During several raids conducted by militia combat patrols, federal troops had been captured who begged for their lives, claiming that they were not loyal to the federal government but had been forced to serve in the federal units because their families were being held hostage. In some cases, the men claimed that their families would be denied food and water if the men did not join the federal forces; but in other cases, they were simply told that their families would be executed outright.

After careful and thorough questioning, it was determined that many of these men appeared to be telling the truth. They were not traitors but in some cases were patriots who had put into an untenable position because they had been unable to escape from the federal occupied territories. Donnelly knew that his troops were uncomfortable with summarily executing fellow Americans unless they were truly traitors, and he agreed with their concerns. So it was decided that henceforth federal troops who surrendered and were Americans would be transported to the Van Zandt County prison in Canton where they would be questioned. If the interrogators believed they were being forced to fight for the federal government, they would be segregated and treated well. Other captives who were thought to be actual traitors would be tried and summarily executed if found guilty of treason.

The next question was what to do with the prisoners who had been forced to fight for the enemy. If they were released to go back to their families, they would just be forced to return to the fight as part of the federal forces. If they were not released, then the feds would have no reason to continue to provide for their families. That was a serious problem, and a solution had not been immediately determined.

CHAPTER XXXIII

The answer to what to do with prisoners would become more pronounced when the federal forces who had surrendered at Fort Hood were brought to Canton. However, that was not a sure thing when the militia started moving out of the Fort Hood area with not only the prisoners but the tanks, artillery, and antiaircraft guns that had been captured. The attack on the fort had been very successful, but problems were developing to the south that might keep the entire operation from succeeding.

After the special operations unit had taken out the guards along the road from the west gate, their next task was to hit the communications center for the fort and knock it out before an alert about the attack could be sent to the Iranian force to the south. They believed they had destroyed the communications center before it could send any message but had no way of knowing that there was a separate civilian-operated ham radio not far from the base that notified the Iranians of the attack.

Colonel Norman Blake had been elevated to commander of the special operations company that was assigned to contain the Iranian force. The previous company commander had been diagnosed with cancer, and because of Blake's excellent record, he was the logical choice to take command. Four Blackhawks had taken his special operations company and supporting infantry platoon to a landing zone about five miles from the location of the Iranian camp. From the LZ, the team moved cautiously toward an intersection of two Texas state highways a mile north of the enemy encampment. One highway ran north to south and the other east to west.

If the Iranian commander was alerted to the militia attack on Fort Hood, he could quickly move a column north and arrive at

Fort Hood within a few hours. While this might be too late to stop the attack, it would put his armor and troops into a position to hunt down the retreating militia. Blake knew he didn't have enough men and weapons to destroy the Iranian force, so all he could hope to do was do as much damage as possible and slow down its advance.

Blake's unit had landed the night before the attack on Fort Hood so he could have some of his team conduct a careful reconnaissance of the enemy camp. It was a large site that straddled the north-to-south highway, and the tanks and infantry transport vehicles were parked near the highway so they would have quick and easy access to the road. However, it was clear from the way that the vehicles were positioned that they expected to have to head south to stop the expected attack on the reserve center.

This gave Blake an idea. He knew of the approximate time of the Fort Hood assault, so he decided to give the Iranian commander what he was expecting an attack on the reserve center that was just a few miles south of the Iranian command. It was also on the highway and covered six acres. There were several warehouses that housed the large stash of ammunition that the feds believed was the ultimate target for the East Texas militia.

East Texas militia special operations commanders were given wide latitude to adapt their tactics as they saw fit, so the colonel did something that commanders were usually reluctant to do. He split his force. He sent one of his special operations A teams and a squad of infantry with a machine gun and two mortars to launch a diversionary assault on the reserve center. It was to take place an hour before the scheduled attack at Ford Hood, and it was successful. As Blake watched through binoculars, the Iranian infantry brigade and its supporting armor sprang to life. The tanks were all mounted by their crews and moved out with the infantry in support. They were moving south toward the reserve center.

The A team that Blake had sent to launch the fake attempt to take the reserve center included Jamie Donnelly who was now a corporal and a weapons specialist. The team had gotten as close as possible to the reserve center, which was surrounded by thick piney woods and had opened fire on a guard post with its machine gun and small arms while the mortars had fired several dozen high-explosive rounds into the compound. They kept up their fire for several minutes until Jamie spotted a federal unit moving out of the center in a clear attempt to flank the special operations team.

The "A" team was in danger of being cut off from its planned escape route that would take it back to the rest of Colonel Blake's force. Jamie was with three other men of the team under the direct command of Sergeant Willie Jones, who was a heavyset black soldier who had been an army ranger before resigning in order to join the militia. Jones made an immediate decision: he sent one of the members of the team to alert their commander, Lieutenant Robert Cannon, to the danger on the flank. Jones had already decided what needed to be done, he and Jamie and the other team member would attack the flanking enemy unit to cover the retreat of the rest of the team.

Jamie was well aware that this was probably a mission that would not end well, but he did not hesitate because it was his job. When Sergeant Jones ordered Jamie and the other soldier, Private Phillip Goldberg, forward, they immediately complied. Fortunately, despite the fact that it was a moonless night, all A team members had night-vision equipment on their weapons so they could see the enemy movements while not being easily seen themselves. It took just few minutes to get into position, and they opened fire on the flanking enemy soldiers. They took down four of them with their opening volley, but there were at least twenty men in the attacking group, and Jones and his men were taking heavy fire. They were spread out about fifteen yards from one another with Jones in the middle, Jamie on his right, and Goldberg on his left. They were in a thick patch of woods, so Jamie could see Jones through his scope but not Goldberg.

Jamie was equipped with an M16 automatic rifle with an attached grenade launcher. He saw Jones signal him to move forward so he could get in effective range to use the grenade launcher. The sergeant also signaled Jamie that he and Goldberg would provide covering fire while Jamie advanced. The young

Donnelly acknowledged the order and stood up to start moving. However, when Jones stepped out of cover behind a tree to cover Jamie, he was cut down by enemy fire, but Jamie didn't hesitate; he ran forward in a zigzag movement and miraculously avoided the heavy but random fire that was tearing up the trees and bushes around him. Then he jumped behind a fallen tree that gave him some cover and launched three grenades at the enemy positions.

Five federal troopers were killed and three more wounded. In the meantime, Goldberg, who was an excellent marksman, had killed two other enemy soldiers. This was enough for the federal commander; he had lost almost half of his troops and really had no idea how large the militia unit he was attacking was. He ordered his men to stop advancing but to continue firing into the woods at suspected militia positions. This fire did no prevent Jamie from getting back to Sergeant Jones and to find that he had been killed by the incoming fire. Then Jamie checked on Goldberg and found him lying on the ground severely wounded. The random but massive amount of fire laid down by the enemy had been partially successful.

While moving from one tree to another in his effort to get back to his comrades, Jamie had periodically stopped to fire at the federal forces, and this made them continue to think that they were facing a formidable force. The American military had a commitment to the philosophy that no one was left behind dead or alive. That philosophy was also ingrained in the members of the East Texas militia, and while Jamie knew that he could not carry both Jones and Goldberg out, he could at least try to save Goldberg who had become a good friend.

He slung his weapon and reached down to pick up his friend when he felt a sharp pain in his side. He reached down and felt the wetness and knew he had been hit. He took his rifle off his soldier and despite the intense pain fired his weapon toward the federal position where he thought the incoming rounds had come from. He emptied his clip, reloaded, and emptied another clip. Then he quickly reloaded again, slung his weapon, and picked up his friend. He had apparently pinned down the enemy for the time being, and he was able to start making his way back through the thick woods in the direction that he hoped would take him to the rendezvous point where the rest of the team would be assembling.

He just hoped that he would make it because he could tell that he was losing a lot of blood and growing weaker by the minute. He was also trying to ignore the excruciating pain; but fortunately, just as he felt he could go no farther, he saw three of his comrades rushing toward him out of the darkness. When the rest of the team had reached the rendezvous point, Lieutenant Cannon dispatched six men to try to find Sergeant Jones and his men. As three of them approached Jamie, his strength gave out, and he fell to his knees so he could lay Goldberg gently on the ground. One of the first three to reach them was a medic, and Jamie told him to take care of Goldberg first because he had been shot in the chest. While the medic attended to Goldberg, one of the other team members worked to stop Jamie's bleeding. All special operations soldiers received some medical training, and within a few minutes, both Jamie and his friend were stabilized, at least to the point that their bleeding was stopped.

The three other team members had arrived and established a defensive perimeter while their wounded comrades were cared for. Then they made makeshift stretchers using their jackets, and some downed tree limbs, and they carried the two wounded men back to the rendezvous point where they were all extracted by two Blackhawks. Both of the wounded men were flown back to the hospital in Terrell, Texas, and would survive, but the team was not able to recover the body of Sergeant Jones.

CHAPTER XXXIV

In spite of the casualties, the first part of Colonel Blake's plan had been a success. The Iranian commander had moved his force south to defend the reserve center instead of north toward Fort Hood; however, that changed quickly when he received word of the attack on the fort. Now the federal leader had a quandary on his hands. His orders had been clear—he was to protect the reserve center—but now he received new orders to move his force to Fort Hood. Yet while he believed that his men had successfully repelled the attack against the reserve center, he had no way of knowing that there might not be a second attack. He was not aware that the assault had been a diversion. As a result, he made a decision to leave three tanks and two infantry companies behind at the reserve center. The rest of his command would move north, where Colonel Blake and his men were waiting.

The survivors of the team that had attacked the reserve center had rejoined the main militia force and had been deployed near the intersection of the two highways that the federal force would have to go through to move toward Fort Hood. The Iranian commander had his tanks leading his force up the highway with his infantry following in trucks.

For the federal force, time was now critical; and while the commander believed that his column would eventually run into some token resistance, he did not think it would happen until they were much closer to the fort. Thus, he did not slow down his column as it approached the crossroads in order to send out patrols to make sure that there was no ambush waiting in the woods. That played right in the hands of Colonel Blake who had decided to let the first few tanks go through the intersection before Matt Donnelly let loose his array of IEDs that brought down trees in

front the approaching tanks. At the same moment, other IEDS
went off, blowing the treads off the tanks while antitank weapons
destroyed the tank turrets and killed the crews.

On the south side of the intersection, militia mortar crews
opened up a devastating fire on the trucks loaded with troops. As
trucks exploded and men, often on fire, bailed out, they were met
with a hail of bullets from militia infantry and special operations
soldiers on the flank. This kept the enemy closest to the crossroads
from effectively organizing to move into the woods and counter the
militia attack. However, the militia was still heavily outnumbered;
and approximately fifteen minutes after the attack had started, it
abruptly ended. The Texas troops moved out and headed for the
landing zone where the Blackhawks were waiting to extract them.

The team had accomplished its mission. The highway heading
north was now completely blocked because as the first tanks in line
had been disabled or destroyed, the following tanks had moved
into the other lane to pass them before they too were hit. However,
it didn't work because the militia had hoped it would play out
exactly that way, and the second group of IEDs were set off and
disabled several of the tanks in the other lane. The same thing
had happened to trucks that had tried to pass the burning vehicles
on the highway south of the intersection. The direct route to Fort
Hood was completely blocked because not only were there burning
vehicles in the way, but Matt Donnelly's combat engineers had also
used C-4 charges to bring down several more large oak trees to
further block the road.

The Iranian commander inspected the carnage and knew
that it would take several hours for the road to be cleared by his
remaining tanks, pushing the burning armor and large trees off
the road. He had one other option, and he prepared to take it.
He had four undamaged tanks, and they were used to clear the
road south of the intersection so that the remaining trucks carrying
infantry were free to reach the intersection and follow two of the
tanks as they turned west. They would have to move twenty miles
before they encountered another highway headed north. Half of the

Iranian force would take this route while the other half would wait until the first highway was cleared and then proceed.

Unfortunately, for the Iranian commander, the action at the intersection was not finished. Colonel Blake had left half of one of his A teams behind to monitor the reaction of the Iranian commander because the colonel had one more card up his sleeve. When he got the word from the team leader that the Iranians had taken the bait as the remaining members of the A team moved out to join the colonel at the landing zone, Colonel Blake launched the two Apache helicopters that were sitting in the LZ along with the Blackhawks. They were over the intersection within minutes and hit the two tanks leading the column to the west. They hit fast and hard with rockets and cannon fire and knocked out both tanks and several trucks. Then they returned to cover the Blackhawks that were heading back to join the two militia battalions that were retreating to Canton with their captured federal equipment and troops. The Iranian command was in disarray. There was no clear route available for them to move, and by the time a route was cleared, it would be too late for the force to impede the militia escape.

CHAPTER XXXV

The militia battalions received a triumphant welcome as they rolled back into Canton. The tanks and artillery they had captured had being hidden in various locations along the way through Van Zandt County, and the antiaircraft guns were deployed mostly in the area around Canton where enemy air attacks were eventually expected to increase. Preparations had been made to protect the militia members, their families, and the civilian population. Extensive underground shelters had been prepared, warning systems were set up, and evacuation plans were in place to get everyone to safety. The addition of the antiaircraft guns would provide much-needed additional protection, and it did not take long for the militia to train crews to effectively operate them.

The attacks on Fort Hood and the Iranian force trying to relieve it had been amazingly successful. The men were allowed to celebrate their success for a few days, and the homemade wine flowed freely. Then the soldiers had to deal with a harsh reality of their hard-won victory. They had to bury thirty-five of their own who had been killed in the fighting and remember two others, including Sergeant Willie Jones, whose bodies had not been recovered and brought home.

Many of the members of the two militia units had not stayed in Canton to party with their comrades but instead headed home to be with their families. Yet they had all returned to town for the funerals of their fallen brethren. They stood in formation with their brothers in arms while their friends were brought in their flag-draped caskets to their final resting places in a military cemetery set up across the road from the historic downtown Canton cemetery. General Donnelly was at the funeral that was presided over by the militia's chief chaplain, Major Calvin Vickery, a former longtime protestant army chaplain from the Canton area. There was no political correctness required of militia chaplains. That had been enforced in the federal military to the point that all the chaplains had eventually resigned or been forced out of the military. After all, according to the progressives in the new federal order, the Socialist Republic of America was no longer a country based on Judeo-Christian beliefs. In fact, the only religion tolerated and encouraged was Islam.

The interment took over an hour and was ended by the playing of taps and the firing of the traditional twenty-one-gun salute. All the militia members stood at attention and saluted as their comrades were laid to rest. There was not a dry eye among the people assembled, both military and civilian, and this included General Donnelly who was openly weeping. To his men, this was not a sign of weakness but a sign of strength and compassion from a man who would send his men into battle to defend their nation and their freedom but suffer each time one of them died. On this occasion, Donnelly was thankfully able take the time to personally visit with and console each of their families, but some of the people closest to him saw that it was starting to weigh heavily on him.

There were now over three hundred soldiers buried in the military cemetery, and Donnelly feared the worst was yet to come. The price of freedom had always been high. Yet following the funeral, Donnelly had other duties: visit the over four dozen soldiers who had been wounded in the battle. There were three major hospitals in the militia-controlled counties that took care of the men and women units, two in Terrell and Longview, Texas, and the other in Tyler, Texas. Soldiers wounded in the assault on Fort Hood and the Iranian brigade had been transported to all three hospitals.

General Donnelly had already been to Terrell to see his son Jamie and tell him how proud he was of him for not only putting up a great fight but also risking his own life to save a fellow soldier. He was happy to inform Jamie that his friend and the man he saved, Phillip Goldberg, was going to fully recover. The general had also visited the other wounded at the Terrell hospital and their families, but not everyone would make it. Two of the wounded had died and were among those buried in the mass funeral the general had just attended. Now he would go to Tyler and Longview to see the rest of the wounded.

While the general was taking care of his men and their families, his newly constituted intelligence staff now under the command of Ray Thibodeaux had been interrogating the prisoners captured at Fort Hood. Some of them were single men who were obviously hard-core supporters of the new federal government, but many others were men with families, and they all told the same story. They had been forced to fight for the federal government because their families were being held hostage in a detention facility in Mesquite, Texas.

Thibodeaux reported directly to the general and said that he believed the men, and this complicated the original problem of what to do with the prisoners. He now firmly believed that if they were held by the militia, the families would no longer be of any value to the feds and would either be turned out on the streets to fend for themselves and probably starve to death or simply be executed by the feds. If the prisoners were released, then the original scenario would probably occur, and they would be sent back into federal units to fight the militia.

Neither option was acceptable to Ray or the general, so Ray requested that he be allowed to send out a recon patrol to find out the layout of the detention center. The general agreed, and the first patrol was sent out. Once this decision had been made, it was a wait-and-see situation as far as the prisoners were concerned, but that was not the only thing that was occupying the militia intelligence section and recon patrols. Ray Thibodeaux's cousin Daniel and his Donaldsonville, Louisiana, militia had continued to monitor the federal activity in New Orleans. The string of recent defeats of the federal troops had made them more cautious about confronting the militia with anything less than an overwhelming force. As a result, they continued to bring more troops, mostly from the Middle East and Africa, into New Orleans along with more armor and artillery.

However, the buildup was slow because word about the victories of the East Texas militia had spread throughout the county and had once again caused a surge in resistance movements in many other states. This diverted federal resources to other locations and made it difficult to gather the sufficient force needed to take on the East Texas militia. So at this point, there was little the feds could do about the growing power of the Texas forces, but it increased their determination to take some decisive action.

CHAPTER XXXVI

Jamie Donnelly was unaware of any of this as he was recovering in the Terrell, Texas, hospital from the wound he had received while saving his friend, Phil Goldberg, during the battle near the reserve center in South Texas. His wound had been severe, and he had lost a lot of blood, so recovery would take a while. Jamie was not happy about this since he was anxious to rejoin his unit, but there was a plus side to his hospital stay.

He was being well cared for by a beautiful young nurse named Kathy Gilmore. She was twenty-five years old with natural blonde hair and a gorgeous body that was a result of vigorous exercise when she was off duty. She was totally dedicated to her profession and had been honored to be appointed to the rank of lieutenant in the militia medical corps. She had immediately found herself attracted to this young soldier and had often come to visit him during her off-duty hours. She was impressed by the fact that Jamie did not try to use his status as the son of the commanding general to get any special attention. On the other hand, Jamie was impressed by the fact that Kathy was not awed by who he was and was just interested in him as a young man who was fighting for their country.

During her time off duty, she would often spend it with him, mostly talking in his room, although when weather permitted, she would help Jamie into a wheelchair and take him out into the hospital courtyard. The couple would spend even more hours just talking. Jamie told her about his strange odyssey that had led him to this place and this time. He also confessed that he was uncomfortable with the fact that he was being hailed as a hero for doing something that any American soldier would do.

Kathy told her own story that was similar to Jamie's. She had originally revolted against her family and been caught up in the progressive movement. The new federal government had sent her to nursing school, and she believed she was going to be providing health care to the most downtrodden elements of American society. Instead, she found herself in a hospital in Dallas that catered to the federal elite and their families. When the EMP attack occurred and everything was thrown into chaos, people who were being subjected to starvation and disease were flocking to area hospitals but were turned away by the hospital where Kathy worked.

It did not take long for this highly intelligent young woman to realize that the new order declared to exist by the government she worked for was a fraud that was designed to establish a totalitarian government existing only to protect the relatively small group of people who would run this new Socialist country. Everyone else was to be considered little better than slaves. Shortly after the EMP attack, Kathy had gone to her superiors to see if she could get a leave of absence and transportation so she could return to her home town of Forney, Texas, to check on her family. She had not heard from them in weeks and was crushed when her request was denied.

She was informed that her duty was to serve the federal government and nothing else was supposed to matter to her. That was when she started looking for a way to escape; however, without transportation, there was no way she could make the thirty-six-mile trek from Dallas to Forney. Fortunately, she found an unexpected ally when she confided her plight to one of the doctors she worked for at the hospital: Dr. Jarod Reynolds. She did not expect him to help her, but she felt he was someone she could talk to without being betrayed.

It turned out that Reynolds was also planning to escape and most importantly had the means to do so. At this time, Kaufman County, Texas, was still under control of the federal forces. The county included the cities of Forney and Terrell, and there was a federal hospital in Terrell. Since Dr. Reynolds was trusted by the federal forces, he was assigned to spend two days each week at the hospital in Terrell. He was provided with a car and enough fuel to take him on five round-trips to the hospital. Then the car would be refueled for five more trips.

The car was due for a refuel during the week following his conversation with Kathy. Jarod Reynolds was in his fifties and had been a US Army physician who had served two tours of duty overseas during the war on terrorism. When he had been discharged, he had taken a job in Shreveport, Louisiana, where he lived with his wife and two teenage daughters.

He had been attending a medical conference in Dallas when the EMP attack had occurred and had no way to get home. He soon found himself impressed into federal service at the hospital in Dallas. He pleaded to be allowed to return to Shreveport and was promised that he would be as soon as it was possible. However, after several months had passed, he soon realized that it was not going to happen. He decided to pretend to be satisfied with his new status and gain the trust of his superiors. This ultimately led to the situation where he had access to a vehicle to take him to Terrell and then back to Dallas. At first, he was only provided with the fuel to make a single seventy-two-mile round-trip to Terrell. Eventually, it was decided that it would be easier to just fuel the car for multiple trips.

This gave the doctor the opportunity he had waited for— escape back to his family in Shreveport—and after talking to Kathy, he had offered to take her with him and drop her off in Forney before he proceeded to Shreveport. Kathy explained to Jamie that this was the way she had made it back to her family and why she had remained in hiding in her parents' home for almost a year until Kaufman County had come under the control of the East Texas militia. Then she had resumed her career as a nurse, but this time, she was working in a hospital that took care of American patriots like Jamie.

It did not take Kathy's coworkers long to realize that the relationship between the young soldier and the dedicated nurse was going beyond that of a patient and a caregiver. On the day that Jamie was due to be discharged to return to his special operations unit, he proposed to Kathy, and she accepted. They were married in

Forney a month later in a military wedding with General Donnelly and Matt Donnelly in attendance along with the members of Jamie's special operations unit and all the men that Jamie had been with on the escape from New Orleans.

The couple spent their honeymoon in a cabin on the banks of Lake Tawakoni not far from Canton. For a full week, they were able to forget the fact that they were in a war. They made love every day and just enjoyed each other and their brief respite from their duties. Then Jamie returned to his unit, and Kathy resumed her nursing duties. They had acquired a small house in Terrell where Kathy lived full-time and Jamie lived whenever he was off duty. Unfortunately, that was not often because the battle for freedom never stopped and seldom slowed down for long.

CHAPTER XXXVII

During the time that Jamie was recovering in the hospital and falling in love, his special forces A team had not been idle. The recon patrol that Ray Thibodeaux had sent out to survey the federal detention center where many of the federal prisoners captured at Fort Hood claimed their families were being held had returned. The patrol had observed the center through binoculars for two days and confirmed that the camp contained mostly women and children who appeared to be malnourished and suffering greatly.

The recon team also determined that because of the composition of the people interned at the detention center, it was lightly guarded. There was only one understrength platoon of federal guards assigned to the center, and they alternated in working eight-hour shifts. That meant that were only thirteen men actively guarding the facility at any given time. For the militia special forces, this constituted a soft target that could be easily overcome. It was decided by Donnelly and his staff that there were several valid reasons for conducting this raid, the most important of them being the fact that these were American women and children being held by the enemy, whose lives would clearly be at risk if they were not rescued. In addition, it would send out a clear message to the enemy that they could not hold Americans as hostage without severe consequences and would also tell Americans that they did not have to be forced to serve as cannon fodder for the enemy.

A plan of attack was carefully crafted that included three special forces A teams to make the actual assault and a company of militia infantry to secure the perimeter around the detention center while the prisoners were extracted. The attack would also be covered by a diversionary attack against a federal outpost in Dallas County not far north of the detention center. The outpost was a staging area for the troops that patrolled and controlled the city of Dallas and surrounding towns like Carrollton, Farmer's Branch, Garland, and others. It was a large facility and also housed vehicles, weapons, and ammunition; so it had to be protected at all cost.

The facility could be captured by a major assault by the militia, but it would be costly and was not worth the cost in the current environment with East Texas militia trying to expand its control over rural counties and prepare for an inevitable attack on the militia by the federal forces. However, a limited diversionary attack would hopefully keep the federal outpost from reinforcing the detention camp until the prisoners were safely evacuated. Another A team and an infantry platoon were assigned to create the diversion.

Once again, the superior training of the militia and exceptional planning by the staff carried the day. Both attacks were successful, and the families of the federal prisoners were brought back to Canton. The federal prisoners were reunited with their families and provided with food and shelter, but they were also assigned jobs. There were no chances being taken since their loyalty to the militia could not be immediately established, so they were given jobs in the militia in supply and logistics or in the private sector, doing work in the construction of housing or military facilities. None of them would be assigned to combat roles or sensitive areas.

It was assumed by most of the militia members that all the federal forces involved in the defense of Fort Hood had been killed or captured, but that was not exactly true. Five members of the federal force had escaped: four enlisted men and an officer who had led them out through a hole in the militia lines. The officer was Captain Jordan Billings, the American patriot who had provided the intelligence necessary for a successful attack and had killed the post commander and chief enlisted man.

As the attack had unfolded, and it became clear that the federal forces were being overwhelmed, Captain Billings had pulled four men out of the line and ordered them to accompany him. He told them to hide behind one of the buildings while he tried to find a way out. He then walked boldly toward the militia lines with his hands raised in surrender. He was relieved when he was not just shot down, but the militia commander had given his men orders to capture any officers that they could. The captain was taken prisoner but asked to immediately speak to the militia commander.

His request was granted, and when he was alone with the commander, he gave him a password that was immediately recognized. The militia commander had been briefed on the fact that he was to look out for a federal officer who was actually working for the militia. He was to facilitate his escape so he could rejoin the federal forces. As they talked in private, Jordan explained his plan. If he showed up to the federal command in the area as the sole survivor of the attack, he would probably be immediately a suspect; but if he brought other federal troops with him, his story would be more plausible.

The militia commander agreed and called his first sergeant over and explained the situation to him, and the sergeant accompanied Jordan back to a spot near where the federal troops had been told to hide. The sergeant told Jordan to give him ten minutes to clear the area for his escape and then to move his men out. When Captain Billings and his men finally rejoined the federal force, he was hailed as a hero who had managed to at least save a few men from the militia attack on the fort. He was promoted to the rank of major and placed on the staff of the federal area commander. He was now in position to provide even more valuable intelligence to the militia.

CHAPTER XXXVIII

Following the highly successful operations against Fort Hood and the detention center where the families of federal prisoners were being held, the counties controlled by the militia experienced a period of relative normalcy. It was springtime, and many of the members of the militia were sent home to their farms or ranches to plant crops and spend some downtime with their families. The militia continued to send out recon patrols to determine if there were any imminent threats to the Alamo. None were detected, and there were no air attacks on the militia-controlled areas. This actually caused some concern for General Donnelly and his chief of intelligence Ray Thibodeaux. It was almost like the proverbial calm before the storm.

In the meantime, the people of Van Zandt County were going about their business. They were part of a vibrant free market economy that was based partly on the barter system, plus the development of a currency system that allowed people to be paid for the goods and services they provided. The members of the militia were paid for their active service as were the police and firefighters who protected their local communities. Other members of the communities received payment for the food they produced or the services they provided like carpentry, plumbing, or medical and dental care. Since Canton had once been the home of one of the largest flea markets in the world, the tradition continued except that instead being only once a month on the weekend before the first Monday of each month, it now occurred on each weekend.

Similar markets had been in all the militia-controlled counties; and they provided residents with the opportunity to barter their crops, meat from slaughtered livestock, or even homemade wine or liquor for other things they might need or just want. It was a system that worked, and no one went without food, but the same was not true for other commodities like medicine. While local doctors and pharmacies were producing and using natural herbal remedies that could be effective for treating minor illnesses, there was a serious shortage of antibiotics and other drugs to treat the often serious injuries of members of the militia and residents who might need treatment for illnesses like cancer, cardiac, or respiratory problems.

To try to alleviate this problem, Ray Thibodeaux sent out recon patrols to see if there were any vulnerable targets in Dallas where some of the needed drugs could be obtained. They isolated one location: a hospital in Richardson, Texas, a suburb of Dallas that was the primary facility for treating federal troops and the elite civilians who were in control of the occupation of Dallas. In fact, that had been the hospital where Kathy, Jamie's new bride, had been forced to work.

Unfortunately, the hospital was well guarded, and there were too many federal units stationed in the vicinity that could come to the relief of the hospital if it was attacked. The risk was too great, so for the time being, the counties in the Alamo would have to rely on their medical personnel to do the best they could with what they had. However, help came from an unexpected source. There was an Indian reservation in Polk County, which was one of the counties that had recently come under militia control. The Alabama/Coushatta tribes lived on the reservation, and true to their warrior tradition, many members of the tribe had served in the US military through the years. Many of these veterans and other tribe members were members of the Polk County militia that was now part of the East Texas militia.

The tribal shaman, David Lone Wolf, had also been producing large amounts of traditional and often ancient herbal remedies to help his people and other citizens in the area who had little, if any, access to modern medicine. Many of the medicines were found to be remarkably effective in treating certain medical conditions, particularly potentially deadly viruses and infections. The word spread throughout the medical community and surrounding counties and eventually to the doctors and hospitals all over East Texas. While the remedies were not sufficient in all cases where they were used, they were successful enough times to keep David Lone Wolf and his assistants very busy producing them.

The tribe also provided other valuable assistance to the militia. Some of the tribe warriors had been members of special operations units in the military including the Green Berets, Navy SEALs, and marine recon. They easily became integral members of the militia special operations teams. They also had some special skills that had not been taught to them by the military: they were expert marksmen with high-powered bows and arrows that could be used to silently kill the enemy from fairly long range.

Their skills had been used in the recent assault on the detention camp where the women and children were being held. One of the tribal marksmen was Danny Lone Wolf, the son of the tribal shaman. The strike on the detention camp had to be swift and surgical so that the guards could be taken out without having an opportunity to kill or injure any of the innocent women and children being held in the center.

There were elevated guard towers at the four corners of the detention center, and they were each occupied by one guard twenty-four hours per day with the guards assigned to eight-hour shifts. This was perfect for the A teams assigned to liberate the camps because they had four tribal marksmen assigned to the teams. They synchronized their watches at exactly 10:00 p.m., and they all loosed their arrows at the same moment, and all four federal guards died silently. This allowed the other member of the special forces teams to cut through the fence, breach the compound, and quietly kill the remaining guards. The women and children in the camp had been saved.

CHAPTER XXXIX

Several more months of relative calm went by with no direct aggressive action by the federal government, with the exception of more foreign troops and equipment being brought into the ports in New Orleans and Houston. It was a slow buildup and would eventually become a threat, but that had not slowed down the advancing of the militia. Three more counties had come under the control of the East Texas militia that now included territory from the Oklahoma border to just north of Houston. There were now over thirty thousand troops on call for the militia, and the Buchanan family had been joined by dozens of other gunsmiths who were adding to the growth of the militia armament.

All this had not gone unnoticed in Washington DC where the current unelected president of the United States, Richard Thompson, was presiding over a meeting of his military command council. Almost half of the high-ranking officers on the council were representatives of the Islamic states that were the primary allies of the federal government. The extent of the influence and control they had was clear from the fact that Thompson was the third president to be named since the EMP attack. The person who had ordered that attack had been President Jeremy Brandon, a lifelong Communist who had failed in his efforts to drive the American people into complete subjugation.

A significant number of Americans had fallen into the well-orchestrated progressive agenda to get people totally dependent on the federal government for their survival by getting free stuff. Yet there had been many more people who had refused to accept the false allure of Communism since they knew it required them to become subjects of the government and give up the basic freedoms that most Americans still cherished. This had led to the initial resistance to the imposition of the new order, and that resistance had been much stronger than the left-wing leaders had expected. They decided that there were too many people to control, and so their answer was to have the EMP attack reduce the population and allow them to ultimately take control after the deliberately created anarchy subsided.

Initially, the plan seemed to be succeeding with the federal forces being able to take control of the large cities as their populations were reduced by riots, wholesale looting, starvation, disease, and even murder to more manageable smaller populations. However, the problem of continued resistance by certain dissidents was not being resolved; and ultimately, the federal council decided to replace Brandon with someone who would be more ruthless. They chose a former US senator from Delaware, Sharon Thompson, who had been steadfast in her defense of the imposition of the new progressive order on the people of the United States.

She had no problem ordering the federal forces to arrest thousands of Americans, intern them in detention camps, and use drugs to control the inmates. She also was aware that the federal forces were not strong enough to put down rebellions on their own and needed help, so agreements were made with the only countries that had troops available to essentially invade the United States. These were countries like Syria, Iran, Iraq, and Libya that were under the complete control of radical Islam elements. For a high price, they agreed to provide troops to the beleaguered federal government. However, these troops would not serve under the command of a woman, so the federal council forced Sharon Thompson to resign and appointed her husband, Richard Thompson, to take her place. He was even more ruthless than his wife.

He was now the president who was faced with the fact that the East Texas militia was continually winning battles against federal forces and expanding its control over counties in the state of Texas. Despite the best efforts of the feds, they had not been able to stop word of these successes from spreading to surrounding states and eventually all over the country. Thompson and his advisors decided it was time to go all in against the Texas militia. However, they would not make the mistake again of dividing their forces as had occurred during the first attempt to destroy the militia. This assault would be a massive attack from one location.

In Canton, Ray Thibodeaux was receiving intelligence from his cousin Daniel that the buildup of foreign troops and equipment coming into New Orleans was again accelerating. He was receiving similar reports from the recon patrols that were watching the ports in southeast Texas. Obviously, something big was being planned; and several weeks later, Ray received word that large convoys of enemy troops, armor, and artillery were on the move. But much to his surprise, they were not heading north but east. The enemy columns from South Texas made their way to New Orleans and joined up with the federal column waiting there. Then they all continued to move east on Interstate Highway 10 into Mississippi.

Ray and Daniel had both heard that there were small pockets of resistance operating along the Mississippi coast, but no one in Texas or Louisiana had any contact with them. This unfortunately meant that they had lost track of the federal columns. There was no explanation for this movement to the east since the states of Mississippi, Alabama, and even Florida did not have resistance movements powerful enough to warrant this type of attention from the feds.

In fact, the federal units had turned north shortly after entering Mississippi. This was initially unknown to the Louisiana or Texas militia, but fortunately, Daniel suspected that such a movement might be the case and had dispatched several recon patrols to the border between Louisiana and Mississippi. It took almost a week, but one of the patrols finally got information after they had crossed the border that a very large federal force had been spotted going north on a highway near the border.

This information was transmitted to General Donnelly and Ray Thibodeaux. It arrived almost simultaneously with an additional message from Jordan Billings who had been appointed commander of an elite company of federal infantry that had been ordered into Oklahoma to join other units preparing for a major operation against East Texas. The message also conveyed his concerns that this was going to become a major threat to the militia. While the militia leadership was pondering the meaning of this intelligence, they received word from several leaders of the Oklahoma militia that large convoys of federal troops and heavy equipment were moving through Oklahoma toward its southern border with Texas.

What was happening now became clear to both Ray and the general: the columns moving out of Texas that had turned north in Mississippi were probably going to enter Arkansas, turn west, and ultimately join up with the federal troops moving south through Oklahoma. Ray had the Blackhawk Helicopter units transport both militia recon teams and special operations units into southern Oklahoma to determine the potential strength of the enemy force and their possible points of attack. The result of this intelligence gathering was a source of great concern to General Donnelly and his staff. When all the federal units were amassed somewhere across the Red River that was the border between Texas and Oklahoma, there would be a force of almost fifty thousand men, scores of tanks, and dozens of pieces of heavy artillery preparing to attack the Alamo.

It had also been determined by the recon patrols that an airbase had been established in central Oklahoma where three dozen F-16 fighter jets were located along with a significant force of Russian attack helicopters. The bottom line seemed to be that the East Texas militia forces were ultimately going to be attacked by a federal force that would have the militia heavily outnumbered and outgunned.

CHAPTER XL

General Ben Donnelly met with his staff to discuss their options. These were the only people who knew the gravity of the situation, and they all agreed on one thing; retreat or surrender was not an option, so a plan of action had to be formed that would keep the federal forces from utterly destroying the militia and ending the hopes of millions of Americans who wanted to live free and take back their country.

During these meetings, Ray Thibodeaux provided the general and his staff with the updated intelligence from Oklahoma. The federal columns that had moved east from Louisiana and Texas into Mississippi and from there north into Arkansas would be joining up with the federal forces moving into southern Oklahoma within a few weeks. It was clear that the unified force would be heading to the Texas border to prepare for staging of an all-out invasion, and it appeared that they were planning to attack across the Red River. The federal forces were massing along Interstate 75, so it was believed that would take that route to Highway 271 and cross the Red River Bridge into Texas just north of the city of Paris, Texas.

The obvious defensive move was to destroy the bridge and force the federal forces to build a new bridge while under fire from the militia. There was one major problem with this approach, however, because of the lack of rain during the previous year: the river level was low enough at several points to the east of the bridge to allow tanks and infantry to cross without using a bridge. However, most of the staff believed that the destruction of the bridge would allow the militia to heavily defend that crossing. They were surprised when the general suggested that while a plan should be made to destroy the bridge, it might be wiser to leave it intact.

The general pointed out that the federal force would assume the bridge would be destroyed, but if it wasn't, they would probably decide to use both the bridge and the nearest ford downriver to launch simultaneous attacks on the Alamo. In that case, they would be making the same mistake that had led to their destruction in a previous attack: dividing their force. Several staff members immediately pointed out that it would also mean that the militia would have to divide its force to meet both threats.

That was when the general dropped his bombshell that he had an ace up his sleeve that he had not yet revealed to anyone, even to his most trusted staff members. One of the first things that the new federal government had done after the EMP attack was to lock down all military bases in the county. This was simple enough in most cases since the vast majority of bases were under the command of officers who had proven their loyalty to the new federal order.

The attack had wiped out communications outside of the East Coast by rendering the electric grid useless and knocking out batteries and generators that could power phones and computers. This was in addition to the destruction of cell phone towers and Internet communications. However, the federal government had prepared for this, and each base had a radio room set up that would protect long-range radios from the effects of an EMP attack. While the Pentagon had contacted all bases to order the lockdown, there were some bases that did not acknowledge the receipt of the order or confirm the lockdown.

These bases were mostly in the south and included Fort Rucker, Alabama, where army helicopter pilots were trained, and Barksdale Air Force Base in Bossier City, Louisiana, just a few miles east of the Louisiana/Texas border. It was assumed by the federal government that the orders had been received and that a breakdown in communications kept them from acknowledging the orders. With so much going on, it had taken several months before anyone from Washington was able to check on the status of some of these bases.

Barksdale was a very important base where originally several squadrons of the aging, but still powerful B-52 bombers were located along with three F-16 fighter squadrons. The military cutbacks by the government had reduced the number of planes in the air force significantly; there had still been a full squadron of twelve B-52s and a squadron of eighteen F-16 fighters on the base, along with several newer and more powerful B-1 bombers. Fort Rucker was the home of a squadron of twelve Apache helicopters and another of twelve Blackhawks. There was also a large squadron consisting of sixteen A-10 Warthogs, the famous "tank buster" aircraft.

When federal patrols were sent to the two bases to find out why they had not made contact with the Pentagon, they found the bases virtually deserted. Many pilots, their supporting personnel, and their families were all gone as were numerous vehicles and most of the helicopters and aircraft. Also missing were the ammunition, bombs, and rockets that gave the squadrons' awesome firepower. The federal troops that were loyal to the government had either been killed or locked up in buildings on the bases.

They had no idea where the patriots and all the equipment had gone. This caused a panic in the federal command, and an all-out search was launched to find the missing soldiers and the aircraft. It was unsuccessful; hundreds of people along with vehicles, aircraft, weapons, ammunition, and fuel appeared to have just dropped off the face of the earth.

In fact, the planes and personnel were now in and around a new hastily constructed airbase in the huge Angelina National Forest located in East Texas and taking up part of four counties. This large federal-designated area also included the Sam Rayburn Reservoir. This was the result of an elaborate plan that been designed several weeks after the EMP attack by the two base commanders who were preparing to fight the new federal government. It was a laborious process because maximum secrecy had to be maintained. Aircraft from the two bases were flown out one or two at a time to the regional airports in Longview and Tyler, Texas.

These airports had been set up with long runways that could handle large commercial jet aircraft. Since no commercial flights were taking place anymore, the airports were not being used; so they were perfect landing zones for military aircraft including the B-52s, B-1s, F-16 fighters, A-10 Warthog, and helicopters. Once they landed, they were quickly hidden in hangars or dragged into nearby wooded areas where sites had been cleared to provide them with a safe area with camouflage to hide them from any possible air surveillance. However, it was clear to the American base commanders that these airports would be among the places where the federal forces would look when they found out that there were planes and helicopters missing from these major bases.

Every plane and helicopter that was flown out of Barksdale and Fort Rucker contained more than just its crew; they carried the family members of the crews and as much ammunition, food, and fuel as they could hold. The next step was to find a new and secure location where not only the aircraft but the crews and their families as well as the fuel and ammunition could be hidden. The base commanders were in the counties that were already part of the East Texas militia, and they contacted General Donnelly for help. Militia patrols looked at many possible locations and ultimately determined that the Angelina National Forest was the perfect place.

There was an engineer company that had been based at Barksdale, and they were airlifted into the forest to join up with several local National Guard engineer units that had the heavy equipment needed to build not only several airstrips but also bunkers and housing where the aircrews and their families could be comfortable and protected from the elements. It took several months, but eventually, a massive secret military complex was constructed. While it was being built, several more hidden National Guard units came out of hiding to join the militia. They had been in hiding for weeks or even months until the militia had taken control of their counties. The unit commanders knew that they could do nothing on their own but now were in a position to join a large and powerful force.

The National Guard units consisted of a tank battalion, a military police company, and three companies of an infantry battalion. These units were assigned to guard the new top-secret installation being constructed in the Angelina National Forest. Securing the forest for use by the militia did not require a lot of effort. The new federal government had many things on its plate, and dealing with federal parks and forests was not a priority. The control of these sites was left in the hands of the park rangers, and as was the case in many of them, the rangers at Angelina National Forest were mainly military veterans who had taken the oath of office to defend the Constitution of the United States. They were loyal to that oath and became allied with the militia.

The militia officer assigned to supervise and coordinate this new secret base was Major John Donnelly, the general's son and Jamie and Matt's brother. He was not in command of the base; that was given to Brigadier General Harold Walker who had been the commander of Barksdale Air Force base. The aircraft and crews were gradually moved from Longview and Tyler to the new base, which was to be kept a secret by the base commander and General Donnelly, until now when the militia command staff found out that they were in a much stronger position than they had thought.

CHAPTER XLI

This additional force was strong, but it was not enough to put the odds in favor of the militia in the coming fight. Donnelly had not let his troops on the ground be informed about the complete situation for security reasons, but they did know they were in for a decisive fight that they could not afford to lose. The word of the impending threat to the East Texas militia had quickly spread to other Texas counties and other states. Everyone knew that if the Alamo was taken, the possibilities of a successful fight against the feds would disappear, possibly forever.

The response was immediate. Daniel Thibodeaux and Louisiana militia commanders were aware that the movement of the government troops out of New Orleans to join the federal force massing in Oklahoma had left only sufficient troops to maintain the detention center and occupy New Orleans and a few surrounding parishes. There was no way that the feds could launch any offensive operations in Louisiana, so Daniel felt confident that he could send reinforcements to the Texas militia. He dispatched three infantry companies and a weapons platoon with mortars and heavy machine guns.

In the West Texas panhandle, there were a number of county militia units that effectively controlled their counties primarily because they were sparsely populated, and there was no reason for the feds to spend resources subduing them. However, since virtually every able-bodied man belonged to the militia, they were able to send several infantry companies to East Texas. Other reinforcements came from New Mexico, Arkansas, and Mississippi. None came from Oklahoma, however, because Donnelly had a special job for the two thousand men of that militia.

The Oklahoma militia general David Williams had trained his men with the same intensity that he had learned from General Donnelly's methods, so he had an effective fighting force that he willingly placed under Donnelly's command. Williams was told to essentially make his force invisible. They were not to try to ambush or harass the federal forces building up on the Oklahoma/Texas border but were to wait until the battle was joined. Then they were to move in behind the federal forces, cut off their supply lines, and launch swift surgical strikes against the feds from their rear.

Donnelly had a plan that he hoped would give the militia a good chance of not only beating back the attack by the federal forces but doing devastating damage to the feds that would put them on the defensive. The plan involved an elaborate ruse that was one of the techniques that Donnelly was famous for. Matt Donnelly and his engineers were ordered, with the help of civilian contractors and two infantry battalions, to construct defensive positions south of the bridge across the Red River from the area where the federal forces were expected to attack. In fact, federal troops had already been allowed to secure the bridge after a brief firefight with token opposition from the East Texas militia.

The defensive positions being built by the militia would involve entrenchments for the infantry and redoubts for the placing of artillery, antiaircraft guns, and tanks that would be close enough to the bridge to provide heavy fire on the enemy as they tried to cross the bridge. However, the positions were also close enough that they could receive fire from enemy artillery and tanks deployed along the north bank of the river. Many of the men building the trenches and redoubts wondered about the wisdom of this since the militia was sure to be outgunned, but they were under orders, and the general had always made the right calls so far.

In fact, only Matt and several of his officers know the truth. These defensive positions were going to be occupied but only by fake artillery, tanks, and antiaircraft weapons. These were being constructed at a location outside of Canton and while made up of logs and plywood and would look like the real thing from the air. The general was also well aware that the feds had spies planted within the militia ranks, and at least one of them had been identified as a member of one of the infantry battalions involved in the construction. His movements were being carefully monitored by two members of Ray Thibodeaux's intelligence unit who were attached to Matt's engineers.

The spy was a private named Leroy Jones who had showed up at the western border of Kaufman County several months earlier. He claimed to be a US Army veteran of the 101st Airborne who had escaped from Dallas and wanted to join the militia. He had federal identification papers and an expired Texas driver's license that appeared to confirm that he was a US citizen from Texas who was living in a federally occupied area. Unfortunately for him, when questioned about his military history, he was talking to a real veteran who had served in the 101st Airborne and knew that the information conveyed by Jones about the company he served in was incorrect. This was reported to Ray Thibodeaux who shared it with General Donnelly, and the two men decided to accept Jones into the militia and possibly use him to provide false information to the enemy.

That was precisely what happened when the two members of militia intelligence followed Jones late one night to the bridge over the Red River where they used their night-vision goggles to watch him pass on some papers to two federal soldiers. The militia intelligence operatives believed it was a map of the positions that were being prepared by the militia. Jones was allowed to return to the militia position without being arrested but would continue to be watched in case he could be used again.

The actual militia defensive positions were being built by other units approximately three miles south of the false positions. They would be out of range of any federal artillery along the river but would be in a perfect position to open fire on the federal troops and armor moving toward the phony defensive entrenchments. The troops building this second position were led to believe that they were constructing a fallback position in case the forward trenches were overrun. The militia intelligence operatives had someone inform Jones about this and also let him know that the forward positions were under orders to hold their fire until the main federal armor units had crossed the river. They were supposed to do this even though they would possibly receive some heavy incoming preparatory fire from the federal positions.

The intelligence operatives followed Jones once again and watched as he delivered this new information to his federal contacts. The next step in the ruse was to find a way to make the advancing federal forces believe they were actually receiving fire from the forward positions of the militia that had survived the federal barrage. Matt Donnelly and his engineers were assigned that job, and he decided to set up a number of sites with C-4 charges that would be detonated as the federal troops advanced, and that would appear to be caused by incoming artillery fire. This would hopefully convince the feds that there had been severe damage caused to the militia forward trenches.

The ruse would also include the use of good old-fashioned fireworks. There were several former fireworks distributors in Van Zandt County who had traditionally sold their wares during the weeks preceding the July Fourth weekend and the New Year's celebrations. After the EMP attacks, the dealers gave their remaining inventory to the militia to use it as it saw fit. Matt determined that the fireworks could be used in the militia emplacements to create the impression that there was artillery and machine gun fire coming from the phony militia trenches.

However, several members of Matt's engineers would have to put themselves in harm's way to pull this off. Two men would be in foxholes near the C-4 charges so they could detonate them as the enemy advanced toward the false militia entrenchments. Three more engineers would have to survive the federal bombardment of the militia front lines and then set off the fireworks. When Matt told his men that he needed volunteers for these highly dangerous missions, they all volunteered.

CHAPTER XLII

The militia's defensive plan was coming together, so it was time for General Donnelly to have General Harold Walker and Donnelly's son John flown to the Canton headquarters so that they could determine how the use of this large secret reserve force of planes, helicopters, and tanks could be effectively deployed against the enemy. General Walker and his staff came in two Blackhawk helicopters to Canton and were greeted personally by Generally Donnelly and his chief of intelligence Ray Thibodeaux. They arrived late in the evening and were welcomed by the general who was particularly happy to see John who he had not talked to in several months. As they embraced, John whispered in his father's ear that they needed to meet privately.

The general knew instantly that something was wrong, so he hosted a dinner for General Walker and his staff where they talked in general terms about the defensive deployment of Walker's command, but Donnelly told Walker that they would go into specific details at a meeting the following morning. In the meantime, Donnelly told Walker that he wanted to spend some time with John and his brothers since they had not seen John for many months, and his son Jamie had not seen him for years. The general took his three sons to his private office that was located in the Van Zandt County courthouse in downtown Canton.

The general sat down behind a massive antique oak desk, and he had John sit in a chair facing him, but he had Matt and Jamie stand next to him behind the desk. He handed Jamie a pad of paper and a pen. The general asked John how his daughter-in-law, Melissa, and two grandchildren, ten-year-old Allison and fourteen-year-old John Junior, were doing. His son told him that they were well and happy. However, this small talk was a cover because the general and his other two sons were carefully watching John who was rapidly blinking his eyes in Morse code that he had learned as a Boy Scout along with his brothers. They had been taught by their father.

Jamie recorded the message his brother was sending on the notepad, but it was not necessary because his father and brother were both reading it correctly. John informed them that Walker had gone over to the enemy and that the secret base had recently been seized by federal forces. The families of all the American soldiers and airmen, including John's wife and children, were being held separately and were hostages to force their spouses to do the bidding of the feds. John also informed his siblings and father that he was wired so that Walker and the officers who were with him, who were also feds, would be able to overhear his conversations. It was audio only, so there was no video to be concerned with.

As the four men continued to talk about seemingly trivial matters such as family stories and memories, John was also handed a pad and pen so he could write notes to his siblings and fathers while continuing their conversation. The general asked his son what he thought of General Walker, and John immediately took the cue. He praised Walker and said that his command was ready to effectively support the militia in the upcoming battle with the feds. While he was talking, he was writing on the pad and drawing a map of the base, showing where the hostages were being held, where the loyal American troops were being guarded, and where the feds were housed. He also highlighted the locations of all the federal guard posts.

John's notes outlined the plans of Walker and the federal force. They knew of the impending attack on the militia and that Walker's command would be an integral part of the militia defense, so since Walker knew he would be briefed on the defenses of the militia and his assignments to provide support, he would be able to give that information to the federal command. He would then use his control over the hostage families to force the pilots, aircrews, and armored units to attack their fellow Americans in the militia from the rear and participate in the final annihilation of the East Texas militia.

Since John was the official liaison between the militia and the force commanded by Walker, he had to be brought to the meeting in Canton, but it was made clear to him that his family would be immediately executed if he betrayed the federal plans. That was the reason he was wired with listening devices. However, since John was being held prisoner with the other American officers on the base, he informed them before he left that he might be able to convey a secret message to his father about the plight of the patriots and their families. They were unanimous in urging him to try to get a rescue operation launched against the base immediately. Otherwise, the American soldiers and airmen would launch a desperate attempt to overpower their guards and take back the base.

They knew that there was very little chance that they would succeed and that they and their families would probably be killed, yet they were determined that they would never be forced to betray their country and attack their fellow American soldiers. Ben Donnelly now knew exactly what he needed to do, and he wrote a note to John, assuring him that everything would be taken care of. He then informed his sons and the federal troops who were monitoring them that he hated to cut their visit short, but he was scheduled to meet with several of his special operations commanders who were supposed to depart with their teams in Blackhawk helicopters to be dropped over the Oklahoma border to recon the buildup of the federal troops.

No such operation was scheduled, but the general was definitely going to meet with his special ops teams to prepare them for another mission. Donnelly had suspected that his headquarters was being monitored before John had revealed that information to him, so he had taken some precautions. He had told Ray Thibodeaux to be in his separate office in the courthouse and await instructions. As soon as the meeting with his sons ended, Donnelly went to Ray's office and told him what was going on and what needed to be done. He also gave Ray the map of the militia base that John had drawn.

Ray immediately put four special forces A teams on alert as well as two combat infantry platoons. He arranged for a meeting to take place between the general and the A team commanders. It would be held out in the open so that the federal spies monitoring the activity of the general would be able to see it take place but not be able to hear what was said. The team commanders were given the map of the militia base so that they could plan a coordinated attack that would save the American hostages, release the American soldiers that were being held prisoner, and secure the aircraft and armor that were essential for a possible victory against the federal force attacking from Oklahoma.

Since Donnelly had been suspicious from the beginning and conveyed his concerns to Ray, the security chief had assigned several four-member security teams to monitor the movements of General Walker and the five staff members he had brought with him, as well as the two pilots of the Blackhawks that had brought them to Canton. The pilots had gone to their assigned quarters for the night, but two of Walker's people had been seen outside of the courthouse and were clearly the team that had been listening in on Donnelly and his sons. The other three men had been followed as they made their way to a position where they could watch the movements of any militia aircraft.

The militia security teams did not interfere with Walker's men but carefully watched them. The two men outside the courthouse were seen following the general and his driver to the airfield where he met with Colonel Norman Blake, who was in charge of the operation, and his A team leaders. They had a brief discussion, and then the team leaders led their men to board the four Blackhawks. The federal spies watched this, and they saw the choppers take off and head north toward the Oklahoma border. The spies had not seen the two infantry platoons that had boarded three other Blackhawks kept at another secret location and had already taken off.

They had flown east, and as soon as the flights carrying the special operations teams knew they were out of sight of anyone in Canton, they also turned east, rendezvoused with the other

Blackhawks, and then the entire force headed south toward Walker's base.

Jamie Donnelly was onboard one of the helicopters with his A team still commanded by Lieutenant Cannon. However, this mission was like no other for Jamie because he was being sent to rescue three people he had never even met. His sister-in-law, Melissa, and his nephew and niece, John and Allison, were being held hostage and were in serious danger. He would not let his brother down.

CHAPTER XLIII

The map provided by John Donnelly had pinpointed a landing zone for the helicopters about two miles from the captured militia base. Colonel Blake and his team leaders had come up with what appeared to be a good plan of attack despite having to prepare it in just a little over two hours. There were four specific points of attack. The first priority was to secure the area where the militia family members were being held; the second was to take over the area where the militia pilots, tank crews, and other American military personnel were imprisoned. The next two points of attack were the airfield where the planes, helicopters, and armor were positioned and the encampment where the federal troops not on guard duty were stationed.

John Donnelly had told his father that the mostly lightly guarded target was the area housing the families of the American soldiers since there was little threat of these noncombatants attempting an escape. On the other hand, more federal troops had been assigned to guard the compound where the American airmen and soldiers were being held. There was also a smaller federal force assigned to guard the airfield; but there was a concern that in case of an assault on the base, these troops would try to destroy the planes, helicopters, and tanks rather than allow them to fall back under than control of the militia. This was something that had to be prevented.

The East Texas militia force knew that it was outnumbered. John Donnelly had told his father that there were over two hundred federal soldiers guarding the base and that most of them were foreign fighters from Iran, Syria, and Libya. John had also informed his father that they were assigned to eight-hour shifts so at any given time only approximately one-third of the force would actually be on guard duty. That meant that the guards on duty had to be silently removed so that the main federal forces would not be alerted.

To accomplish this, Danny Lone Wolf was sent in with ten warriors from the Alabama/Coushatta reservation who were experts with bows and arrows. Other members of the special forces teams were equipped with silencers for their weapons that had been made by the Buchanan family. The attack plan called to two A teams to be assigned to secure the families being held hostage while two more would liberate the area where the captured American troops were detained. The two infantry platoons were divided, with one full platoon and two additional squads assigned to attack the federal barracks where the off-duty federal troops were assigned while the other two squads would secure the airfield.

The militia force set down on the landing zone and despite operating in the dark quickly made it to the base, where they got a surprise. The base was brightly lit up, which would not have been done by a secret militia base. This was another confirmation that federal troops were completely in control of the base. However, it also gave the militia troops an advantage since they could clearly see their targets. The initial attack was to be done by the special operations units to rescue the hostages and free the American troops. Lieutenant Cannon was in charge of the two A teams assaulting the tent city where the hostage families were being held.

The federal forces did not believe there was much risk of the families trying to escape, so there was only a reinforced squad of ten men patrolling the perimeter that was loosely secured by hastily strung barbed wire. The area was brightly lit by solar-powered spotlights, but the good news was the cleared area that contained the tent city was surrounded by thick woods that allowed the militia teams to get very close to the patrolling guards. It was also a plus that the guards were mostly just standing around in sight of one another, so there was little movement. This made it easier for the militia to approach their positions. Danny Lone Wolf had four of his archers with him, and he used hand signals to assign them to take out four of the guards. Cannon also used hand signals to assign five of his marksmen with silenced weapons to eliminate the other five guards.

They all synchronized their watches and timed their attack to take place at exactly 3:15 a.m. when the other two special operations teams would be hitting the area housing the captured American soldiers. Danny Lone Wolf and his team along with the other special forces personnel did their jobs with perfection. The guards all went down within seconds of one another. Cannon then led the teams into the tents and were relieved that their biggest fear had not materialized. There were no guards inside the tents. The militia members were in the process of waking up the rescued families when they heard gunfire from elsewhere in the camp. They didn't know where it was coming from, but it was a clear indication that something had gone wrong.

The problems had occurred when the additional five Alabama/Coushatta warriors and other members of the special forces teams were moving toward the barracks where the American soldiers were housed. This part of the camp was different from the area where the hostage families were incarcerated. These were secured barracks, not tents, and a larger cleared area around them. There were also twenty-five guards instead of ten, and there was something else involved that the militia did not know about until it was too late. In the unlikely event that any of the captured soldiers was able to penetrate the barbed wire fence surrounding the barracks, there were trip wires outside that were hooked up to grenades. One of these was set off by one of the Indian archers that were moving into position to take out a federal guard. The young warrior was killed instantly by the exploding grenade, and it alerted not only the guards in the immediate vicinity of the barracks but also federal personnel that were off duty and asleep in the main area of the camp.

The firefight at the compound housing the American captors was brief, because although they were slightly outnumbered, the militia special operations personnel were highly trained marksmen who made short work of taking out the federal troops. However, this did not solve the main problem facing the reinforced platoon that was assigned to attack the sleeping federal force that was off duty. The feds came pouring out of their barracks and split into two groups, half heading to the sound of the fire at area where the American soldiers were imprisoned and the other half moving toward the airfield where they might try to destroy as many of the helicopters and aircraft as possible to keep them from falling into the hands of the American militia.

The American infantry commander, Captain Mark Ryan, a thirty-year-old former army ranger, knew that this could not be allowed to happen; but at the same time, he needed to protect the soldiers and their families. The federal troops had been hit hard by the militia infantry, but the divided force that was making its way toward the airfields and the rescued American captives had considerable firepower. The first thing Captain Ryan did was dispatch three of his squads to go after the federal troops moving toward the special forces teams preparing to extract the soldiers and their families. If they could hit the federal forces from the rear, his infantry should be able to alleviate the pressure on Lieutenant Cannon and his men.

Ryan had radioed Cannon to inform him of the threat heading in his direction and then sent two of his remaining three squads to assist the men at the airfield. However, the squad leaders were told to hold back until they received orders from Ryan. He had alerted the young sergeant, Alvin Grant, in charge of the two squads at the airfield of the impending threat. The militia squads had been assigned to capture the airfield but not to move in until the American hostages had been secured. However, when they heard the gunfire break out in other parts of the camp, Grant knew he had to move, so his men had immediately attacked the federal forces guarding the airfield; and since there were only ten guards, they were taken out quickly, but one militia soldier had been killed and two others wounded.

Now, Grant was faced with the fact that he had only fourteen men to defend the airfield against an approaching federal force estimated to number over forty troops. Captain Ryan understood this and told Sergeant Grant to deploy his troops and their two machine guns to defend the perimeter of the airfield and to fire smoke grenades to mark the positions of the approaching federal force. Then Ryan contacted Blake about the situation, and he agreed to order two of the Blackhawk helicopters into the attack to defend the airfield. The pilots easily spotted the smoke laid out by the infantry and put down a devastating fire with their 50-caliber machine guns. Most of the federal force members were killed or wounded, and the rest were taken out by the two infantry squads. There was no quarter for these federal troops since they were not Americans who were being forced to fight for the government; they were foreign mercenaries, and they were killed outright.

The situation at the other side of the camp was different because while the airfield was a good distance from the main camp, the areas where the American troops and their families had been held were much closer, and Blackhawks could not be deployed because their fire might kill their own people. Therefore, the defense was entirely in the hands of the four special forces teams. As a part of one of these teams, Jamie had a special assignment: find his sister-in-law and his niece and nephew. As he had entered each tent in the hostage compound, Jamie had called out for the Donnelly family and had received his reply in the third tent. He had just identified himself to his family members when gunfire erupted near the tent.

Jamie took his family members out of the line of fire and into the nearby woods where they were protected along with other militia families by several members of the special forces teams. Once they were safe, he returned to the fight to help save other families. Most of them had been evacuated into the woods, but he could see that the feds were in the process of surrounding the first tent where they had some families pinned down on the floor of the tent with three militia fighters trying to hold off nineteen federal troops who had taken cover behind some parked vehicles. Jamie was still in the cover of the tree line and on the enemy's flank so he could see them but they didn't see him.

Jamie could see that his three comrades could not hold off the attackers for long, and they would soon die along with the families pinned down in the tent. Jamie knew he had to do something quickly, so he slung his M16 over his shoulder and pulled two hand grenades out. His plan was to charge out of the tree line and throw his two grenades at the enemy, then unsling his rifle, hit the ground, and open fire on the feds. He was aware that his was probably a suicide mission, but the lives of other American women and children were hanging in the balance.

However, before he could initiate his heroic but probably suicidal plan, he was joined by Lieutenant Cannon and three other members of his team. Cannon put his hand on Jamie's shoulder and said, "Do you really think we would let you be a hero all by yourself, Sergeant?" "Good to have you onboard, Lieutenant," Jamie replied with a smile. "You have more help than you think," said the lieutenant as he got on the radio and gave a one-word order, "Execute!" He then ordered Jamie and the other team members to attack the federal troops. As soon as they opened fire, militia infantrymen hit the feds from the rear. It was a skillfully coordinated attack that killed all the enemy soldiers and ultimately made sure that all the American hostages had survived.

The rest of the federal fighters had been efficiently dealt with by the A teams that had liberated the captured American soldiers and airmen. Some of the recued soldiers had been provided with weapons captured from killed federal troops, and these men assisted the militia in destroying the federal troops attacking the compound where the military hostages had been held and then going after the force that had bypassed that area and gone after the hostage families.

The operation had been a success since all the American prisoners had been saved, the aircraft and tanks had been captured, and when things had started to go wrong, mortar fire from the militia infantry had destroyed the federal communications center before it could alert anyone of the attack. However, thirteen militia soldiers had died and fifteen more had been wounded.

CHAPTER XLIV

General Donnelly had been awake all night, waiting for confirmation that John's family was safe and the important militia base had been secured. The success signal was received shortly after four thirty in the morning and provided relief for him and his son Matt, but it would be later in the morning before they could convey that information to John. That was also when the next problem for the general and his staff would occur. They had promised to brief Walker and his staff on the militia defense plans in the morning and how Walker's aircraft and other forces under his command would fit into the plans.

There were two ways this could now be handled. The first inclination of General Donnelly when he heard that the militia now controlled the base was to just arrest Walker and his team. However, if Walker did not report to the federal commanders, that would probably alert the federal command in Oklahoma that the militia would now have the resources of Walker's airbase back under militia command. To prevent that from happening, Donnelly decided that the best plan was to conduct the briefing with Walker and his staff and basically lie to them.

They were told that the principal line of defense would be just south of the bridge over the Red River. There would be a fallback position, but the defense would be at the line closest to the bridge where the federal troops would initially be allowed to cross the river and then engaged. Walker's team would not be told that the militia command knew about the other river crossing that the feds would be using to attack the militia and that it would be defended. The important thing was that this false information be conveyed by Walker to the federal command, but that obviously would not happen if he was arrested by the militia before he ever left Canton.

Therefore, Donnelly decided that General Walker and his staff would be allowed to board their helicopters after the briefing and head back to the militia base, which he would believe was still under federal control. This was done in the hope that while onboard the choppers Walker would make use of the fact that he was in the air, and closer to the federal command in Oklahoma he could easily make his report before arriving back at his base. If he did not take advantage of that opportunity and chose to wait until he returned to his base, the communication would never be allowed to happen since he would be arrested the minute the helicopters landed.

The first clue that the plan was going to work was when John Donnelly, who had flown in on the general's helicopter, was assigned to the other helicopter for the return flight. Obviously, Walker did not want to communicate with the enemy in a situation where Donnelly's son John might overhear him. Ray Thibodeaux had his intelligence team plant microphones in both of Walker's helicopters that would be monitored by a militia Blackhawk flying well behind Walker's aircraft and using a cloaking device to avoid being detected by the radar on the enemy choppers.

Shortly after Walker's aircraft left militia airspace, the crew of the militia Blackhawk monitored a transmission from the helicopter containing the general that gave the false militia defense plans to the federal command and confirmed that the aircraft and troops under Walker's command would attack the East Texas militia from the rear. This was what Donnelly needed, and when the two helicopters landed, they were immediately surrounded by militia troops and Walker and his staff were taken into custody and ultimately transported back to Canton for intense interrogation.

Prior to boarding the helicopter, John had said good-bye to his brother Matt who had slipped a note to him, informing him that his family was safe. Upon landing, John was taken to them by Jamie, and he learned from his wife and children that Jamie had saved them. John had always loved his brother even when he had gone against the family and supported the new federal government, but now he knew that Jamie was truly home and was a hero.

Meanwhile, General Donnelly was immensely relieved by the fact that Walker had been arrested, but he was bothered by the question of why a general in the US Air Force would willingly betray his country. Under interrogation, Walker admitted that it was his ego that had been damaged because when he agreed to transfer the assets he had at Barksdale Air Force base to East Texas, he assumed that he would be in total command and was not happy that he was to be under the command of General Donnelly. However, he claimed that this was not the reason that he had agreed to cooperate with the federal command. Before the feds had approached him to betray his country, they had taken his family hostage.

Ironically, Walker's family had been rescued by the members of the American militia that he was planning to betray. He had authorized the detention of the families of hundreds of American soldiers and airmen who had been willing to sacrifice themselves and their families to defend freedom. Since Walker had not been willing to resist the federal demands on him, he would ultimately be tried for treason, but that would come later.

The first concern for General Donnelly and his command was to defeat the impending attack that would be coming in days. He had appointed his son John to command the military units that had formally been commanded by General Walker. The first thing John did was to order the armor units and their supporting infantry to Canton where they were then deployed to the river crossing downstream from the bridge over the Red River where the main federal attack was to take place.

Secondly, John sent his helicopter units to the airport in Tyler, Texas, and his fighter jets, bombers, and A-10 Warthogs to the airport in Longview, Texas. That put them in a position to make immediate responses to the coming federal assault. Ray Thibodeaux had concluded that based on the information his intelligence units had uncovered, the federal attack would occur on midnight in two days. For the massive number of militia that were preparing for the fight, it was a nervous time. They were not being lied to by their commanders. The militia knew they were going to be outnumbered and outgunned, yet they prepared to make what might be the final stand of the best chance for America to regain its freedom.

General Donnelly wanted to raise the morale of his troops by letting them know that there was additional air power and armor support that would be coming to their aid, but he had to do it at the last minute so the information would not fall into the hands of the enemy. He was confident that the feds were not aware that the militia had taken back the base in South Texas, but he wanted to do something more to lure the federal forces into the trap that was being prepared for them. Ray Thibodeaux had the solution: militia private and federal spy Leroy Jones was still being carefully monitored and used by the militia intelligence to provide false information to the federal forces.

Once the construction of the forward trenches and redoubts that were part of the ruse being prepared to lure the federal troops into the trap was completed, Jones had been transferred to another unit that was doing routine construction on what was supposed to be a forward airfield near the Red River where militia Blackhawk and Apache helicopters from Canton were to be stationed. Jones was not aware of the false artillery and tanks that were being constructed in the original trenches, so he was allowed to meet with his federal contacts and inform them of the airfield.

This ruse was designed to do two things: confirm to the feds that there were no additional aircraft available to the militia and provide them a target where no militia aircraft would actually be deployed. After this contact, the battle on the Red River was imminent, and Jones was no longer of use to the militia intelligence, so he simply disappeared. However, the information he had provided was critical to the plans of the federal commanders. They had set the attack of the ground forces to begin at midnight, but they could not risk having all their armor and infantry cross over a single bridge; so the armor would use the bridge, and the infantry would cross the river in small rubber boats. This would be combined with other infantry and armor crossing the river downstream at the ford. All this would be preceded by a heavy artillery barrage on the militia forward positions, but that would only come after a daylight attack by federal fighters on the forward trenches and the fictitious airfield.

Donnelly knew that in order to be effective, the federal airstrikes would have to occur during the late afternoon prior to the midnight assault by the ground troops. So early in the morning, he went to the front and met with his commanders to make sure that everyone was on the same page when it came to the defensive deployment of all militia troops. He also told them to inform their troops that they had more backup than they previously knew about. They were told that if they saw fighter aircraft coming from their rear, they needed to know that it was friendly support, and tanks coming from behind them were also friendly.

Because of the results of the EMP attack, the militia had limited long-range radio capability, but the Oklahoma militia had eyes on the sky that reported via a series of short radio transmissions from one outpost to another that a force estimated to include thirty federal fighter jets was coming in from the north. John Donnelly immediately ordered the eighteen F-16 fighters under his command to intercept the federal fighters. It appeared to be a mismatch since the militia fighters were clearly outnumbered. However, the National Guard and regular air force pilots were highly trained and many of them were combat veterans while most of the federal pilots had received the usual minimal training and only two of them had combat experience.

The result of the air battle was decisive: two American planes were shot down, but the militia fighters took down sixteen enemy fighters, and most of the rest of the federal planes withdrew. The militia couldn't stop them all, and four made it to the American forward position, and two fired on the phony artillery emplacements and empty trenches while the other two attacked the bogus militia airstrip. Then they headed back to their base in Oklahoma, but two of the planes were ultimately shot down when they ran into the returning American fighters that were headed back to their base in Longview, Texas. The American pilots then landed and were quickly rearmed and refueled to prepare for their next mission.

This disaster in the air alerted the federal commander to the fact the militia had aircraft he did not know about, but he still had no reason to believe that the South Texas base had been retaken by the militia and that he no longer had an attack force that would hit the militia units from behind. In addition, he believed that his aircraft had done some damage to the militia positions, and he also still believed that his ground forces had a massive advantage over the East Texas militia, and so at 11:30 p.m., he ordered his massed artillery on the north bank of the Red River to commence their bombardment on the American redoubts and trench line. The feds had sent forward observers across the river, and they were using night-vision equipment to direct the artillery fire. They were too far away to detect that there were no American personnel in the positions, but they were able to report that there were secondary explosions in the area that indicated the artillery fire was not only destroying enemy artillery but also setting off their small arms ammunition and artillery rounds.

Three of Matt Donnelly's best combat engineers were actually setting off fireworks to simulate these secondary explosions. Some of the fireworks had been in the false militia positions and had been set off by the federal air assault and subsequent artillery fire. However, Matt had wanted to make sure the ruse was successful, so more fireworks had been set up about one hundred yards behind the phony American positions. To the federal forward observers, these were close enough to the area being bombarded to convince them that the explosions were in the militia positions and were being caused by the federal artillery bombardment.

The explosions were being set off by Greg Forney, Douglas Brennen, and Tony Mitchell, three noncommissioned militiamen who had volunteered for the job. They were dug into foxholes where it was hoped they would be safe from the federal bombardment. They had wires buried that would allow them to set off the fireworks remotely. Some of the remote detonations worked, but as was feared, some of the artillery rounds fired by the federal artillery had overshot their target and destroyed some of the wires leading to the fireworks.

This required the three engineers to set off all the fireworks they could remotely and then move forward toward the federal artillery impact area and set off the other fireworks manually. They had to try to dodge the federal artillery fire that was still raining down on the faux militia positions. Greg Forney (a short but agile young man from Shreveport, Louisiana, who was the son of a former army ranger) and Tony Mitchell (a former college student at Southern University, a predominantly black college in Baton Rouge, Louisiana) went in quickly. Both men had been members of their local militias and had escaped to East Texas when their units were disbanded because of the threat of them being uncovered. Both of these young men had become excellent combat engineers in Matt's unit and did their jobs effectively, setting off their firework displays that helped confuse the federal forces.

Unfortunately, their friend and comrade in arms, Doug Brennen, a young man who was proud of his heritage as a descendant of an Irish American family that that migrated to New Orleans in the mid-1800s, was killed by a federal artillery round almost immediately after leaving his foxhole. The thirty-two-year-old sergeant was survived by his young wife and two small children. Despite this devastating loss, the militia plan had worked: the federal commander believed that between the limited air raid and massive artillery barrage, he had neutralized most of the militia force that was capable of opposing his assault. He ordered his tanks and troops to begin crossing the river and move to the attack. He also ordered his units at the ford downriver to commence their crossing. These units were to be deployed to attack the right flank of the militia positions, and they were not expecting any opposition to their crossing. In fact, the armored battalion from the treasonous General Walker's former command had been deployed just south of the ford along with another militia tank battalion and two infantry battalions that included a heavy weapons company with mortars and antitank weapons. The south bank of the Red River ford had also been heavily mined by another group of Matt Donnelly's engineers.

The crossing of the Red River Bridge had been unopposed by the militia, and within two hours, there were over fifty tanks over the river along with two brigades of federal infantry. The tanks were deployed in three separate lines with federal infantry units following each group of tanks. They moved forward toward what they believed were the militia positions that had been bombed and hit hard by federal artillery. They expected to meet minimum resistance, but they almost immediately ran into unexpected trouble. Mason Williams and Gregory Jordan were both sergeants in Matt Donnelly's combat engineer battalion. Both had military experience in demolitions and now were hiding in separate foxholes not far from the fake American entrenchments.

They had participated with other engineers in placing antipersonnel mines and IEDs loaded with C-4 explosives across the line of attack being used by the federal troops. The mines were contact mines that were set off by pressure, so unfortunately, many of them were set off by the tanks and no real damage was done. However, there were numerous mines, so not all were run over by tanks, and many of the rest were stepped on by members of the federal infantry. Many of them were killed or wounded. At the same time, Williams and Jordan were remotely detonating the IEDs to damage the tanks, and they disabled eight of them.

This slowed the federal advance down but did not halt it, and the second wave of tanks and infantry had been moved into position to cross the Red River at the bridge and join in the attack. This appeared to be a good sign for the success for the federal force, but it never happened because in addition to the combat engineers that were setting off the charges that were slowing the federal advance, there were six other members of the militia hidden in foxholes not far from the bridge. They were special forces troops with lasers. After the initial federal movement across the river, these men watched as the second wave of federal forces was massing on the north side of the Red River and informed General Donnelly's headquarters who, in turn, ordered the commander of the airbase at Longview to launch four fighters to destroy the bridge. The fighters had been rearmed with rockets, and 20mm ammunition and with the use of the laser-guided targeting deployed by the special operations troops took out the bridge with one attack.

While this was occurring, the federal troops and armor crossing at the ford downriver had been met with unexpected heavy opposition from the militia. Their attack had ground to a halt at the same time that the federal force attacking in the west had reached the militia positions and found that they were unmanned and that there were nothing but dummy artillery and armor positions at the site. The federal force did not know what it was facing, so the commander ordered all his units to hold in place until daylight when they could get an idea of what the militia strength actually was. He also ordered all his armor, artillery, and infantry units that were to have crossed the now-destroyed bridge to head east and cross at the downriver ford.

This was exactly what General Donnelly had hoped for, and as dawn broke the following morning, all hell broke loose on the federal units. The militia artillery opened fire on the federal armor and infantry that had crossed the river on the bridge the night before. The federal units could not retreat back toward the destroyed bridge, so the advance was halted, and the federal force moved back a few hundred yards until it was out of range of the militia artillery to wait for the rest of the armor and infantry to cross at the ford and come to reinforce them. The crossing would not take place until just before dawn, and it would take at least four more hours for the reinforcements to join the main force south of the river. That was assuming that they could overcome the surprising strong militia force that had fought the initial federal force at the ford to a standstill.

The column of federal tanks and infantry that had crossed the river at the shallow ford in the middle of the night had not expected any opposition but had sent an infantry squad across the river first to conduct reconnaissance of the area immediately south of the crossing. This type of recon activity was something the militia was prepared for. The combat engineers had not set any of the mines to be detonated by contact, but instead the engineers were in deep-covered foxholes in the area; so when the time came, they could detonate the mines remotely. They were not detected by the federal recon patrol, and neither were the militia tanks nor infantry hidden from sight a mile away from the river ford. They were behind a sparse tree line, but large sand berms had been constructed to hide them, and they were camouflaged so they could not be spotted from the air.

When the federal recon patrol signaled the all-clear, twenty-seven tanks, eight Strykers, and two dozen Humvees, along with two brigades of infantry, started to cross the river. After most of the force had made the crossing, the hidden militia engineers started detonating the IEDs and mines. Tanks were being disabled when their treads were blown off and some Strykers and Humvees were totally destroyed. The infantry was also hard hit with over one hundred men being killed or wounded. This all occurred before the militia armor and infantry moved in for the kill. They did not have the tanks or infantry to match the federal force; so they made a quick surgical strike hitting the federal force with heavy fire, destroying more tanks and other armored vehicles, killing more infantrymen, and then withdrawing into the darkness. This left the commander of the local federal force totally bewildered. He did not know how strong the militia force was that had just attacked his units or where they were now. He just knew that his command had suffered significant casualties in a location where they had been told there would be no militia opposition.

He sent a radio message about his situation to the overall federal commander, General Thomas Moreland Jr., a traitor who had once been in the US Army as a supply officer but had been facing a court-martial for secretly stealing military equipment and supplies and selling them on the black market. He was saved by his father, US senator Thomas Moreland Sr. of New York, who was a key supporter of Richard Thompson who had become the president and ultimate dictator of the former United States of America. The senator had convinced the president that the charges brought against his son had been political and had been orchestrated by his superiors in the military who felt that their oath of office to defend the US Constitution was superior to any oath they had been ordered to take to obey a dictator.

Moreland ultimately convinced the president that his son was an expert in military strategy and tactics and should be in command of the federal attack on the East Texas militia. He also convinced Thompson the political appointment of son to this command would earn the president the permanent support of the powerful group of politicians controlled by the older Moreland.

In fact, the younger Moreland knew nothing about military strategy and tactics but was heavily relying on the advice of his executive officer, Colonel Jordan Billings. The colonel had several men on his staff that had been planted by Ray Thibodeaux, and they were his link to Ray and the militia. As the attack plan on the militia was developed, details of that plan made their way to Ray Thibodeaux and General Donnelly. That was how they knew of the strength of the federal forces, the planned point of attack across the bridge, and that the feds had discovered another crossing site downriver from the bridge. This made it easy for the militia recon units to locate the site.

When Moreland received word that his force at the ford had been attacked, he turned to Billings for advice. He was told to have the troops on the south side of the ford hold in place until the rest of the force arrived from north of the bridge. Then he suggested they move slowly and carefully south until they reached a highway that would lead them to a point where they could attack from the right flank of the militia that had penned down the federal forces that had crossed on the now-destroyed bridge.

Moreland asked Billings why he thought the troops crossing the ford should waste time heading south and then west instead of just immediately heading west on the highway along the river that would get them to the other federal force faster. Billings told Moreland that he suspected that since the militia had somehow discovered the crossing but had only managed to oppose the federal forces with a relatively small force of their own, they would probably have expected the federal advance to take the shortest route to the main federal force and the militia would probably have it heavily mined and have possible ambushes set up along the route. Billings argued the more southern route would be safer. Moreland took his advice and issued the order. Jorge Ortega had been in the command center when this decision was reached. He was one of the two men who actually were militia members working for Ray Thibodeaux. Ortega went immediately to the secret radio that he had hidden outside of the command post and sent a coded message to the militia command post that had been established just south of the main but still-undiscovered militia defensive line.

The stage was now set for an epic battle. The militia forces in the west had ceased firing while awaiting the next move by the federal troops that had crossed the bridge while the militia to the east at the ford was waiting for the federal reinforcements to arrive. General Donnelly met with his staff in the command center just behind the second and real line of defense and assessed the situation. Despite their successes during the night, the militia was still outnumbered and outgunned, at least when it came to ground forces. It was with this fact in mind that Donnelly issued orders for an all-out air assault on the federal forces.

While this air assault plan was being finalized, the militia infantry, artillery, and armor units were nervously awaiting the inevitable attack of the feds to their front. Their morale was bolstered when several militia Humvees passed through their lines and started moving in front of all the deployed troops. The first of the vehicles was flying a flag they all recognized: the 9/11 flag that, as promised, was to be leading them in the fight. With the exception of Jamie Donnelly and Ray Thibodeaux, the flag was still guarded mostly by the men who had months before escaped from the federal detention center in New Orleans. The detachment was under the command of former Navy SEAL George Carson.

At 9:34 a.m., the federal force that had been north of the Red River Bridge when it was destroyed made it to the downriver ford and started crossing the river. The column included forty-three tanks, all the federal artillery, and two infantry divisions with Strykers and armored Humvees. As soon as Donnelly learned that the crossing had begun, he ordered the air assault to begin.

CHAPTER XLV

The militia force had twelve A-10 Warthogs, known as the tank busters, and eight of them were assigned to attack the federal forces crossing the Red River ford. The other four were to support the sixteen Apache helicopters that were going in to attack the federal armor that had made it across the bridge. This was a risky operation because the federal troops were equipped with surface-to-air missiles that could take down Apaches. The Apaches could come in fast and hard, but they still were vulnerable to small arms fire and especially to surface-to-air missiles. To protect them, General Donnelly ordered four special forces teams to move forward close to the federal positions. Their job was to protect four mortar platoons that were also going forward, along with six pieces of militia artillery. They opened fire on the federal infantry just as the Apache helicopters and the A-10s were moving in for the attack.

The combination of the 81mm mortar fire, the militia artillery fire, and the machine gun and automatic weapons fire of the special operations teams forced the federal infantry to hit the ground and destroyed much of their ability to engage the helicopters and Warthogs. The result was a devastating attack on the federal armor. Sixteen tanks were destroyed along with thirteen Strykers and armored Humvees.

At the same time, the other Warthogs were hitting the tanks at the Red River ford. Fourteen more federal tanks were destroyed, but this did not stop the federal force from continuing its advance. It then fell into the trap laid by Jordan Billings that had directed it to the southern route, and militia tanks and IEDs did more damage to the advancing federal force. However, the remaining federal armor and thousands of infantry troops eventually were able to link up with the remnants of the main force south of the Red River

Bridge. They were preparing to attack the militia positions when the militia B-52 and B-1 bombers came in.

They were equipped with five-hundred-pound bombs that destroyed tanks and other armored vehicles and killed hundreds of federal soldiers. There was now complete chaos among the federal troops, and that was when Donnelly ordered the ground attack. His armor, artillery, and infantry drove the enemy back toward the Red River where the retreating federal troops were forced to abandon their tanks and other vehicles in order to join the infantry and swim across the river. However, they found no safety because the Oklahoma militia under the command of General David Williams was waiting for them on the north side of the river and killed many more of the enemy. Even the remnants of the federal fighters could not help because they were once again met by the militia jets and their superior pilots and were either shot down or forced to retreat. The same occurred with the Russian attack helicopters that the federal commander had held in reserve and now employed in a final but futile attempt to turn the tide.

During the ambush of the federal force that had crossed at the ford earlier that day, something had occurred that provided a great deal of satisfaction to the members of the Donaldsonville, Louisiana, militia. The companies dispatched by this militia to assist in the defense of East Texas was led by the militia combat commander Frank Hebert, but he was joined by Daniel Thibodeaux, who felt like this was a fight he had to be a part of. He owed that not only to the people of Donaldsonville but to his cousin Ray.

As the militia ambush of the federal force unfolded, Daniel was in charge of one of the Louisiana militia platoons that were supporting the armored battalions striking the federal column. It was designed to be a fierce but quick fight since the militia knew they were not strong enough to successfully sustain a long battle. The primary attack was being carries out by militia armor, but the infantry was heavily involved, and their job was to fire on trucks containing the federal infantry and cause as many casualties as possible.

Daniel's platoon was heavily engaged with the federal infantry who were leaving their vehicles that were being shot to pieces when Daniel saw someone he immediately recognized. The officer in charge of the infantry in the column was Omar Shala, who was still masquerading as Colonel Raphael Ortega, the man who had ordered the massacre of innocent civilians in Donaldsonville. Things quickly became personal for Daniel; he pointed out Shala to some of the other troopers and told them to concentrate their fire on all the federal troops near Shala but to leave the enemy colonel to him.

His men complied, and Daniel watched as one enemy soldier after another went down under the intense fire. Shala was in a panic as he tried to organize his men to return fire, yet the rest of Daniel's platoon had been informed of what was going on, and they all concentrated their angry fire on the men with Shala who they suspected had likely been with Shala in Donaldsonville. Several of the Louisiana militiamen had grenade launchers, and they used them to blow up the trucks that the federal foreign fighters were using for cover. This fire drove Shala out in the open, and this gave Daniel the opening he wanted. He was an excellent marksman and took careful aim on the vicious Islamist. His first shot knocked Shala's AK-47 rifle from his hands, and his second shot took out the man's left knee, causing him to collapse to the ground and leaving him unable to walk.

Daniel now had a clear path to Shala; so he drew his Bowie knife that had been handed down through his family for years and ran straight at the man that had brutally ordered the killing of so many men, women, and children in Donaldsonville. Daniel's men fanned out to cover him because they knew what was about to happen. Within seconds, Daniel was standing over the man he had seen leading the attack on Donaldsonville and who he thought he would never see again, and he watched with great satisfaction as he writhed on the ground in pain. When Shala saw the militiaman standing over him holding the biggest knife he had ever seen, this so-called brave jihadist who willingly ordered the slaughter of innocent women and children and sent his own men to their deaths was now begging for his life.

Daniel knelt down beside him and said simply, "Where I am about to send you, there will be no virgins waiting. You will just burn in hell!" Then Daniel used his knife to gut Shala like he would a wild hog. He deemed that appropriate, and then he ordered his platoon to withdraw with the other militia units, and he left Shala to die the slow and painful death that he deserved.

When the federal commander, General Moreland, learned that his units were in a catastrophic retreat, he decided to abandon his soldiers and save himself. He ordered his command post evacuated. He knew that he would be initially blamed for the debacle but felt that he could successfully shift the blame to his chief advisor, Colonel Jordan Billings, for giving him bad advice. Unfortunately for Moreland, Billings and two of his officers were missing from the command post, so Moreland had no choice but to get in the Humvees with his staff and personal guards and head north. They had only gone a few miles when the convoy was ambushed by a large force of Oklahoma militia.

The firefight was fierce but relatively short since the militia force was being supported by Lieutenant Robert Cannon's special operations A team. Jamie Donnelly was with the team. He was now a section leader, and he and the soldiers under his command were firing at the federal convoy guards when Jamie saw a lone man sprint from the convoy and head into the surrounding desert. He ordered two of his section members to pursue the individual. They quickly captured him and brought him back to Jamie. He immediately recognized the rank on the collar of the captive and knew that his men had taken the man they were after: federal general Thomas Moreland Jr.

After the militia had destroyed the remainder of the federal convoy, Cannon and his team took Moreland to their nearby Blackhawks and flew him back to the militia headquarters in Canton. Ray Thibodeaux had returned to Canton and personally interrogated Moreland. He quickly determined that Moreland was a coward who was willing to order other men to fight to the death but was not ready to put himself in harm's way. In order to keep himself from being executed for treason, he agreed to tell Ray about the deployment of federal troops in states neighboring Texas, including Louisiana, Mississippi, Arkansas, Alabama, New Mexico, and Arizona. These troops were supposed to capitalize on the imminent defeat of the East Texas militia and destroy the militias that had blossomed in these other states.

Ray sent out envoys to the militias in all these states so they could prepare for the coming assaults. However, the attacks never occurred because after the massive defeat in Texas, the feds were not about to embark on any other operations in the adjacent states. In fact, as had occurred previously, the word of the victory in Texas had spread rapidly through the rest of the country, and state militias had increased in strength and were threatening federal control everywhere. President Richard Thompson and his cabinet decided that they could no longer defend each state, and they were fearful of the power of the East Texas militia, so it was decided to pull all remaining troops out of Texas and the nearby states and send them to reinforce the federal forces in other states.

Within months, the East Texas militia had incorporated other county militias into a statewide force that controlled all of Texas. The states of Mississippi, Louisiana, Alabama, Arkansas, New Mexico, Oklahoma, and Arizona were now free states and had chosen their own governors. All of them were in agreement that they needed to unite into a new but much smaller United States of America. Everyone agreed that the military commander of all the state militias would be General Ben Donnelly.

When the governors of the states met in Canton two months later, they decided that General Donnelly should also be the president of the new United States. Donnelly told the governors that he was honored by the request but adamantly refused. If he accepted the appointment as president while he served as the military commander, he would be establishing himself as a military dictator, which he had repeatedly said was totally unacceptable to him. However, he urged the governors to not tinker with the Constitution but to continue with the election of civilian authorities at the local and state level and have the populations of the states elect members of a national Congress and a president.

The states and counties—or, in the case of Louisiana, parishes—would continue to maintain their own militias but would be subject to the command of General Donnelly when a combined effort might be needed. The feds were back on their heels and were clearly not in a position to launch any significant attack on the seven states that now made up the new United States. However, General Donnelly and his staff did not believe that the war was over and, in fact, did not want it to be over. There were forty-two more American states out there that were still under the thumb of a totally corrupt and brutal dictatorship, and the general felt that the job would not be over until all the states were back in a united USA.

CHAPTER XLVI

The people of the newly constituted United States of America then overwhelmingly chose Texas governor George Michaels to be the new president. Michaels was a former Green Beret captain in the US Army who had organized militias in six counties in southwest Texas. The large city of El Paso was controlled by the federal government that was assisted by drug gangs from Mexico and Middle Eastern terrorists who had been allowed to freely cross the border.

There were little that Michaels and his small militia force could do for the people in El Paso where rape and looting by the enemy were out of control and Americans were dying on a daily basis as a result of starvation and disease. However, Michaels and his men were determined to keep this cancer from spreading into the surrounding rural counties. He had followed the example made by General Donnelly in the eastern part of Texas and had built his force with a nucleus of military veterans supplemented by well-trained civilian volunteers.

They did not have the manpower or the weapons to engage in pitched battles with the federal troops and their ruthless allies. However, the militia under the command of Michaels had something the feds didn't have: they had cavalry. Southwest Texas was ranch country, and if the ranchers weren't using horses in their day-to-day operations, they were raising horses to sell to other ranches.

The traditional regiment of the United States Cavalry consisted of ten companies with approximately one hundred men in each company. Two companies constituted a cavalry squadron, but that was later changed to having the regiment divided into three battalions of three companies each with the tenth company being a smaller headquarters company. Michaels used this original designation but set up the companies to consist of sixty men each commanded by a militia captain. A squadron consisted of three companies and was commanded by one of the company commanders who were designated as the senior officer that would command the squadron when it went into battle. A regiment was commanded by a full colonel with a lieutenant colonel as the executive officer or second in command. Militia majors were in charge of the regiments' supply and logistics support and the intelligence gathering operations.

It was not easy to put an operational cavalry regiment together, because although most of the people in southwest Texas knew how to ride, the horses had to be specially trained to not panic at the sound of gunfire. It took expert horsemen to accomplish this, and they worked diligently so that within six months of the EMP attack, there was a full regiment of cavalry operating in the area. This regiment provided Michaels with the opportunity to use his cavalry as dragoons, who were historically infantry that while moving from place to place on horseback actually dismounted to fight on foot.

When the federal troops started sending patrols into the militia-controlled counties, they were met by squadrons of cavalry that would dismount and set up ambushes that would disrupt the federal advances with IEDs, mortar fire, and machine guns and automatic weapons. Once the attacks took place, the cavalry troopers would mount their horses and disappear into the rugged southwest Texas terrain where federal vehicles could not follow.

This led to the destruction of the federal alliance in southwest Texas with the Mexican drug cartels. They saw no chance of being able to sell their drugs in small Texas towns if they could not even reach them, so there was no reason for them to sacrifice cartel soldiers in an ongoing battle. The Middle Eastern terrorists felt the same. They wanted to get to the major oil fields in West Texas and control the oil supplies in order to finance terrorist attacks in large cities. The chances of that happening quickly were being diminished by the unrelenting militia activity and the apparent inability of the federal troops to take control of any of the counties north and east of El Paso.

This caused the feds to virtually cease any offensive activity outside of El Paso for several years and allowed General Michaels to strengthen his militia force to three full cavalry regiments. Then the federal commander received word that there was going to be a major attack on the East Texas militia and that his force was to be heavily reinforced by foreign fighters with tanks and artillery that would be landed on the west coast of Mexico and brought to El Paso so that he could conduct a simultaneous attack on the West Texas militia.

The federal commander, General David Simmons, was formerly a Far Left member of the US House of Representatives who had consistently voted for any legislation that would weaken the US military and destroy the morale of the troops. Since he considered himself an elitist with superior intelligence to the underlings in the armed forces, he thought as a military commander he could secure the support of the southwest Texas Indian tribes that had once controlled southwest Texas. This included the Lipan and Mescalero Apaches and the Comanche tribe. After all, he reasoned they had once fiercely fought against the US Army, and he was going to offer them the opportunity to do so again. However, he had two problems. First was the fact that the Indian tribes had suffered just like millions of other Americans both before and after the EMP attack. The leftists who had taken over the government and destroyed the American republic had used minorities in the country essentially as cannon fodder, promising things that they never intended to deliver to get the support of the communities.

Since the elitists that controlled the government did not plan to ever hold another free election, the minority votes no longer mattered. The feds would continue to recruit members of the communities into the federal military, but those who did not immediately comply were abandoned and left to fend for themselves. The southwestern Texas Indian tribes had expected this and had made themselves self- sufficient, using many of the ancient skills that they were supposed to have forgotten. They did not trust this federal government, but the tribal leaders were not surprised when General Simmons approached them to join the federal forces.

However, Simmons had another problem because he was not aware that all the tribal leaders sitting around the table in his office in El Paso were US military veterans, and true to the warrior spirit of their ancestors, they were now loyal to the fighters that were trying to save the United States. They were aware of the growing resistance in East Texas, and they were all secretly members of the West Texas militia under the command of General Michaels. In fact, most of the tribes' warriors were excellent horsemen who had quickly become an important part of Michaels's cavalry command.

The tribal leaders listened to Simmons as he proposed making the warriors part of the federal force and providing significant financial incentives to them including relocating all the families to a special facility in El Paso where they would be well cared for. The tribal chiefs knew that this was double-talk for placing the families in a concentration camp where they would be held hostage to ensure that the warriors fought for the federal cause. After some private discussions among themselves, the chiefs agreed to do what the federal general wanted, and Simmons told them that since their reservations were all located in the counties controlled by the militia, the tribes would have to gather at the border of the federal-controlled El Paso County.

There they would be met by a federal convoy of trucks that would transport the families to the facility near the city of El Paso and would take the warriors to a federal training base not far away. The operation did not go as Simmons had planned. As the federal convoy approached the heavily guarded border, there was no sight of the tribe members; instead, the border guards were, in fact, militia troops who had seized the border crossing the night before and donned the uniforms of the federal soldiers. They opened fire on the lead elements of the federal convoy that included trucks and Humvees that were transporting a platoon of federal infantry that was to supervise the transfer of the tribe members into the numerous empty trucks that comprised the rest of the convoy. The militia unit at the border was not alone; as it opened fire, other units of Michaels's cavalry hit the feds on both sides after emerging from concealed positions in the surrounding hills.

The attacking cavalry included the members of the Apache and Comanche tribes who gleefully participated in the total destruction of the federal convoy. The warriors and their families were now totally committed to the militia and were relocated in towns and cities throughout West Texas where they were welcomed with open arms. Collins was now in a position where he could not risk making any further major assaults against the West Texas militia. This was the situation for months until the federal government decided to use El Paso as a base to launch a second front to support the ultimately ill-fated attack on the East Texas militia.

The plan involved two Iranian armored brigades and three infantry brigades landing on the Pacific coast of Mexico and moving to El Paso. From there, they would strike north through the counties controlled by Michaels's militia. The federal plan was to destroy several key cities held by the militia because they expected little serious opposition from the militia cavalry. They might be effective in limited engagements with infantry but were not believed to be equipped to inflict any real damage on armored columns.

Unfortunately for the feds, General Michaels was a lot like his counterpart that commanded the East Texas militia. There were things that Michaels kept from everyone except the key members of his staff that had a need to know. Right outside of El Paso was Fort Bliss, the second largest US army base in the country. It was originally the home of the US Army First Armored Division and a heavy-combat aviation brigade that consisted of forty-eight Apache attack helicopters and thirty Blackhawk helicopters. Some of these helicopters were actually in nearby National Guard and army reserve units, which trained at Fort Bliss for two weeks every summer. The same was true of the First Armored Division that had over 220 tanks either located at Fort Bliss or assigned to National Guard and reserve units.

CHAPTER XLVII

Prior to the EMP attack, Fort Bliss was targeted by the leftist federal government to be dismantled as part of the reduction of the military and its consolidation into a force loyal only to the new order and not to the Constitution or the American people. Part of this process was to replace all the senior officers on the base with federal officers who were willing to oversee the destruction of the finest military force in the history of the world. The new base commander was a former employee of the Department of Justice that was totally corrupt and had been for a long time. Her name was Maxine Williamson, and she had no military background at all; but she could be relied upon to do as she was told with no questions asked, so she was now a general in the federal army.

The other senior officers on her staff were mostly recent recruits into the military who were given commissions based solely on their willingness to serve the government. They had received more and better training than many of their counterparts at other bases but did not really understand the basic organizations of the military units they were to be in charge of. When they took over the command of Fort Bliss, they were supplied with inventory lists of the tanks, aircraft, artillery, vehicles, and weapons on the base. This information had been provided by Major Patrick McMillian, the base S-4 in charge of supply and logistics. He was a patriot, and he knew he was not completely trusted by the increasingly leftist commanders of the military. He also knew that his days were numbered before he was transferred out of the base and ultimately thrown out of the military.

He had decided to do everything he could to disrupt the new government's plans to complete the destruction of the United States. The first thing he did was to submit a totally false report to the new post commander that understated the number of weapons, armor, and vehicles on the base by a full one-third. Of course, the federal commander, General Williamson, and her staff checked on the accuracy of this inventory and to their surprise found it to be truthful. This was because there were many other patriot soldiers on the base and in the West Texas National Guard, reserve units, and newly formed county militias. Over the course of the previous two years, they had been engaged in helping the people of Texas prepare for a new war of independence.

The plan was elaborate and risky but proved to be highly successful. During the summers, when the National Guard and reserve units would come to the base for their two weeks of annual training, they would bring with them their own equipment and vehicles including tanks, Humvees, and Strykers, as well as their individual crew-served weapons. However, when the units completed their two weeks and left, things were different. For example, when a National Guard armor unit from Midland, Texas, came to Fort Bliss, it would not have a full company or battalion complement of tanks that a regular active armor unit would have, but it would have some additional equipment when it left. So if the unit came in with six tanks, it would leave two weeks later with nine or ten tanks, plus a few extra vehicles, weapons, and ammunition.

All this occurred during two summers with many units involved, but after the EMP attack, the federal government quickly moved to rid the major military bases of all members of the armed forces not totally loyal to the government. The National Guard and reserve units were also being disbanded and their equipment retrieved for use by the federal forces. However, much of the equipment in the hands of these West Texas units had mysteriously disappeared as had the unit members and their families.

There had been a hidden base quietly built in the mountains north of El Paso where all this stolen military equipment was stored. The soldiers blended back into the populations of their towns and cities. Since the EMP attack had destroyed all their records of military service, they could not be identified by any federal authorities who might be looking for them. Many of these veterans joined the militia but were instructed not to talk to anyone about the hidden cache of arms. In fact, most of them did not know where the cache was since they had not been directly involved in hiding it. Only a few people were privy to this information, and one of them was General George Michaels.

General Michaels had been effectively using his militia cavalry for years to deter the federal occupation of the counties under his control but knew that at some point his relatively limited group of fighters might be confronted by a federal force they could not handle alone. That finally occurred when Michaels learned from his intelligence sources that the attack on his counties was to occur when other federal forces were moving to East Texas to conduct the assault on General Donnelly's force.

He could not permit this to happen, so he decided to activate all the National Guard and reserve units and bring their heavy armor and weapons into action. He put Patrick McMillian in charge of gathering the unit members and retrieving their equipment. McMillian had joined with Michaels and his militia after he had received orders transferring him to another base. Within a week, the units had assembled at a single location in the foothills of the mountains where the secret base was hidden.

The addition of the armor units and the National Guard and army reserve infantry gave General Michaels a welcomed addition to his cavalry force, but they were still going to be outmanned by a more heavily armed federal force. If the militia took them on head to head on open ground, the best they could hope for was to do serious damage to the feds before having to retreat to escape complete destruction themselves. That was unlikely to happen, so Michaels had to come up with another plan, and he was helped by the Indian tribal chiefs. As was the case with many tribes, many members who had served in the military had been in the special forces as army rangers and Green Berets or in marine recon units, the Navy SEALs, or air force special operations teams.

The federal force was gathered at a hastily constructed encampment just a few miles from the border of the counties controlled by the militia. This was designed to put the feds into a position to launch a quick decisive strike into militia territory that would lure the militia into a battle where it could be destroyed and clear the way for a continued advance into West Texas. Charlie Whitehawk was the Comanche chief, and he felt like he could form the tribe members who had special forces backgrounds into a cohesive unit that could penetrate the federal encampment and cause enough destruction to disrupt the federal force and open it to attack by the militia.

This proposal provided Michaels with a way forward to do what he had hoped to do: put the federal force on the defensive instead of having to place his militia on the defensive. The plan had to be made and executed quickly because it was clear that the feds were preparing to make their move. The plan that was hastily drawn up was put into effect within forty-eight hours. A few hours after the sun went down on a cold desert night, the general moved his units quietly to within a mile of the federal base; and then several hours later, when the enemy troops had gone to sleep, Charlie Whitehawk led his special operations group consisting of thirty-seven men divided into four teams into the encampment. They took out the guards with the use of bows and arrows, or team members used their knives to silence the guards.

The special operations soldiers then attached explosive devices to the treads of enemy tanks that could be remotely detonated. They also set up many claymore mines and IEDs that could also be remotely detonated. The special operations personnel then took hidden positions along the edge of the enemy camp and set up machine gun positions so they could detonate the explosives at the same time they placed direct automatic small arms weapons fire on the enemy encampment. When General Michaels received the radio transmission from Charlie Whitehawk that his mission had been a success, he ordered his 81mm mortar teams to move forward. Once in position, the mortars would initiate the attack by firing on the federal positions.

The mortars opened fire at 3:00 a.m. and targeted the tents that housed the federal infantry. Scores of the infantry troops were killed or wounded in the initial assault, but the rest moved forward to support the tank crews who were running to mount their vehicles. They were decimated with the combined claymore mines and IEDs set off by Whitehawk's teams and the heavy machine gunfire laid down by other members of his teams. Simultaneously, the explosives attached to the treads of the federal tanks were set off by the militia members, and many of the federal tanks were now useless.

At this point, Michaels sent his own armor and infantry into the attack. The attack was swift and furious with the militia tanks concentrating their fire first on the undamaged enemy tanks. There were only five federal tanks that had been manned by their crews, and they never got a chance to open fire before they were destroyed. Some of the militia armor continued to concentrate on destroying the federal tanks while the rest supported the militia infantry moving in and putting heavy fire into the Iranian infantry; that initially was in a state of total confusion. The militia was inflicting heavy casualties on the Iranians, but their commanders were well trained and were organizing an effective defense. The problem for the militia was that they had one brigade of troops attacking three brigades of enemy infantry.

The plan had never been to wipe out the Iranian infantry but to reduce the number of enemy tanks; do as much damage as possible to the infantry, transport, and equipment; and then withdraw before the militia infantry suffered heavy casualties of their own. The militia armor covered the infantry withdrawal, and the Iranians did not try to follow. They were too busy trying to care for their wounded and trying to salvage what was left of their encampment. The fact was that they would never go after the militia force because they were no longer capable of moving to effectively engage the West Texas militia. The Iranian infantry had suffered over seven hundred dead and wounded, and their armor was almost totally destroyed or disabled.

The federal commander also had six attack helicopters at his disposal, but they were in a landing zone near the federal encampment, and two militia mortar teams supported by an infantry company had destroyed the choppers and killed the crews before they get ever get off the ground.

CHAPTER XLVIII

The combination of the disastrous federal defeats suffered in both East and West Texas forced the federal dictator Richard Thompson and his advisors to decide that they could no longer defend their positions in Texas or surrounding states, and so it was necessary to withdraw from the entire area that made up the new United States of America.

However, the withdrawal might not be as easy as the feds planned. When Donnelly got word that the feds were withdrawing, he became concerned, as did Ray Thibodeaux, about the prisoners being held in federal detention centers in all the affected states. It was feared that the feds were perfectly capable of executing the thousands of prisoners prior to the federal withdrawal. Donnelly acted swiftly and decisively by composing a letter that was hand delivered by couriers to the federal commanders in each state.

They were told that the withdrawal of the federal forces would not be contested by the militia if all prisoners in the detention centers were immediately released unharmed. Donnelly told them that if he received word that any prisoners were executed or an attempt was made to take them out of the centers where they were incarcerated and move them to a federally controlled state, the militias in the various states would launch massive attacks against the withdrawing federal troops. Once this information was received by Richard Thompson, he reluctantly ordered the release of all federal prisoners, so he could save what was left of his rapidly diminishing federal forces in these states.

Now, all the Americans in eight states were free, and the newly constituted United States began to function as a free nation. George Michaels was elected president of the new country, and Donnelly used his militia to retake control of the major cities in

Texas and other states. When the federal troops had retreated out of the states, their allies from the Mexican drug cartels had also left because they no longer had federal protection for their operations. However, there were still gangs operating in the cities, and they were given no quarter by the militia. They were hunted down and either killed or arrested. Civil authority was reestablished in the cities, counties, and states.

The new United States government operated as it was supposed to under the original Constitution. It had limited powers that included providing for the national defense, but that defense force was comprised of state militias under the unified command of General Donnelly. The militia members were paid by the state governments, and the counties and towns continued to fund their own police and firefighters. The new national capitol was in Dallas, Texas, and President George Michaels was careful to maintain the sovereignty of the state and local governments. Matters like education, energy production, and health care were left to the state and local leaders to deal with.

There were a lot of things still to be done. There was a vibrant free market economy operating in all the freed states, but there was no unified national currency yet established, and while the states had their local currencies, much of the economy was still based on the barter system. It was working because the vast majority of the American people had learned their lesson. They knew that there was no such thing as a free lunch, particularly if it was to be provided by a centralized government that only provided free stuff to those who agreed to give up their souls to a dictatorial and corrupt government.

Millions of Americans had died as a result of the actions of their own government, but those who had survived had done so on their own and with the help of their neighbors. They would never again vote for leaders who did not believe in the Constitution and the American dream. The problem for Richard Thompson and his dictatorship was that the withdrawal from eight states had not solved his problems. While the feds were able to maintain a strong presence in progressive states like California, Oregon, and

Washington on the West Coast and New York, New Jersey, and Pennsylvania on the East Coast, they were stretched very thin in many other states.

In other states in the West, Midwest, and South, the feds were not able to maintain control when confronted by strong and rapidly growing militias. General Donnelly had the full support of President Michaels in his efforts to liberate other American states from federal control. He put together more highly trained special operations teams that were sent to other states around the country to train their militias in the successful strategies and tactics that had led to the victories by the Texas militia.

Within a year, states like Montana, Wyoming, Nevada, Colorado, North and South Dakota, Missouri, Kansas, Nebraska, Indiana, Georgia, Tennessee, Kentucky, North Carolina, South Carolina, and Florida had achieved their independence. The states had aligned themselves with the new national government headquartered in Dallas, Texas, and despite the danger and logistical difficulties managed in most cases to send senators and representatives to the new national Congress. President Thompson was painfully aware that he was rapidly losing control of his dictatorship. He no longer had the support of the Iranian and Syrian allies in the Middle East who had suffered heavy losses of men and equipment and had nothing more to gain by supporting his government. They also had their own problems to deal with since the Sunni and Shia Muslim conflicts had started up again.

Even the Russians had backed out of supporting Thompson because they were facing an increasing problem of their own from Russian citizens who had once tasted freedom and were willing to fight to bring it back. This all left President Thompson with only one way to control the country: use nuclear weapons to destroy the strongholds of the Texas militia. However, under the direction of Thompson and previous progressive administrations, the US nuclear arsenal had been reduced to just a few nuclear armed missiles located mostly in Nebraska, Kansas, and Oklahoma. These were states that had been liberated, and to keep the nuclear missiles out of the hands of the militia, their nuclear weapons had been disabled by the withdrawing federal troops. The only place solidly in control of the feds that had nuclear missiles was at an ultrasecret base in southern Illinois where there were four missiles that could be fired at Texas and its neighboring states.

However, there would be a problem with the launch because even though the computers that controlled the arming and ultimate launching of the missiles were underground and had survived the EMP attack without damage, the Internet was gone. The failsafe system for the missiles provided for the actual launch codes to be sent from the White House directly to the launch computers located in the bases where the silos containing the missiles were housed. With the Internet down, the launch codes would have to be hand delivered to the missile sites.

This would take some time to get this done, but it had to be handled very carefully with specially chosen men making the delivery. They would know that they would be signing the death warrant for thousands of their fellow countrymen and they were to make sure that there was no hesitation on the part of the men manning the missile site. The attack must take place as scheduled. The man in charge of this was one of Thompson's most trusted officers, General Warren McDonald. The launch codes for the nuclear missiles were kept in a safe in the highly guarded office of General McDonald in the Pentagon.

The codes were not kept in computer files because hackers had been able to penetrate government computers even before the EMP attacks. Since the attacks, even though the limited Internet was still used by the federal government in and around Washington DC, the security of the information stored on them was all suspect. So the codes were handwritten on sheets of paper kept in the safe. Only three people had the combination to it: Muhammed Salam, the president's chief of staff; Admiral Jeremy Walton, head of the military Joints Chiefs of Staff; and General McDonald, in charge of the few remaining nuclear weapons.

To take the codes to the missile silos and make sure that the attack was executed, McDonald picked ten of the most ruthless officers in his and other commands in the Pentagon; their past actions had convinced him that they would have no qualms about murdering massive numbers of Americans. They would be flown to Illinois in a Blackhawk helicopter accompanied by two Apache gunships for security. They would have the copy of the codes in a pouch in the Blackhawk. McDonald accompanied the team to Andrews Air Force base where they would take off on their mission. McDonald shook hands with each of the men and then watched as they boarded the Blackhawk and took off with their escort helicopters. One hour into the flight, the Blackhawk disintegrated in midair because of a massive explosion. Everyone onboard died instantly, and everything onboard was destroyed, including the nuclear missile launch codes.

This was another disaster for the federal government, and as soon as Thompson received the reports, he tried to contact McDonald to get a new set of launch codes sent out. However, no one could find the general, so Thompson sent his chief of staff to access the safe in McDonald's office and retrieve the codes. When he accessed the safe, Muhammed Salam found that it was empty except for a single sheet of paper with three words printed on it: "God Bless America."

Now there was no way to launch the nuclear weapons, and General McDonald could not be located despite an intensive search. As soon as he had seen the Blackhawk take off, he had gotten into his personal vehicle and headed to a safe house in Arlington, Virginia. He was accompanied by Army First Sergeant Aaron Williams who was in charge of the maintenance of all the helicopters at the airbase. He had planted the explosive device that had taken down the Blackhawk. At the safe house, General McDonald and Sergeant Williams made contact with leaders of the Virginia militia, an organization that both men had secretly belonged to for years.

CHAPTER XLVIX

With the threat of a nuclear attack eliminated, US president George Michaels and General Ben Donnelly could continue with their plan to use the extensive and growing militia forces under their command to take back the other states controlled by the criminal federal government and restore the United States of America as it had originally existed. It would be a long fight that would take years, but they were confident in their success because the Americans who had survived the onslaught of the federal dictatorship were united and determined to make it happen.

President Michaels had one request for General Donnelly: he wanted to take the 9/11 flag that still flew over the veterans memorial in Canton and transfer it to the new US capitol in Dallas, where it would continue to be the ultimate symbol of American patriotism. Donnelly agreed but insisted that his militia still be allowed to use it to lead them into any major battle. Michaels understood, and a date was set for a formal ceremony when the flag would be lowered in Canton and transferred to Dallas.

The night before the transfer was to happen, a small group of men met at the flagpole at the memorial. Present were Ray Thibodeaux, Jamie Donnelly, Frank Hansen, William Jackson, George Carson, Billy Jordan, Juan Gonzales, Samuel Bennett, William Travis, Jack Jameson, John McGee, Tim Johnson, and Jerry Calhoun. They had invited General Donnelly and his other sons to join them, but they declined because they felt that this was something this special group of men had to do on their own. They were the group that had escaped from the detention center in New Orleans and had brought the 9/11 flag home.

A strong East Texas wind was blowing on this cool spring night, so when Ray switched on the spotlights that were used to illuminate the flag when a ceremony was held at night, they saw that the flag was whipping straight out from the pole. It had miraculously survived the looting of the Marriott Hotel in New Orleans years before and the American militia battles that had followed. It remained completely intact, and its white and red stripes and blue field with fifty white stars stood out brilliantly. For several minutes, the gathered men just stared at their national banner in complete silence while each thought of the meaning of the flag and remembered their comrades in arms that had died fighting for it. They all thought of Jason Arnaud, the Coast Guard officer turned Mississippi River pilot who had been killed after taking them safely upriver during a dangerous hurricane, and all of them also remembered the individual new friends that they had made since that time who had died fighting by their sides.

Then Ray called them to attention and ordered a hand salute. The men were so caught up in their own thoughts and memories at that point that they were oblivious to the fact that in the darkness all around them over a thousand of their fellow soldiers had gathered and had also come to attention and rendered a hand salute. They were saluting not only the flag but also the men who had brought it home. The men who had taken a simple piece of cloth that that had been discarded as a rag and now been returned as the proud symbol of a revitalized United States of America and had protected it as it led the United States militia into battle. The group included General Donnelly and his other two sons, who were also saluting Jamie, the son and brother they were very proud of.

The flag would now be flying over its new home, the capitol of the United States in Dallas, Texas. It and other American flags would never be allowed to be desecrated or burned again, and it would never be forced to be removed from any site in the name of political correctness. It would be revered and would be symbol of unity and strength, and under its protection, all vestiges of tyranny in the United States would soon disappear forever. "Old Glory" was back!

THE END